Richard Gordon was born in 192
on to work as an anaesthetist at S
ship's surgeon. As obituary-writ
inspired to take up writing full time ....
embark on his 'Doctor' series. This proved incredibly successful and was
subsequently adapted into a long-running television series.

Richard Gordon has produced numerous novels and writings all
characterised by his comic tone and remarkable powers of observation. His
Great Medical Mysteries and *Great Medical Discoveries* concern the stranger
aspects of the medical profession whilst his *The Private Life of…* series takes a
deeper look at individual figures within their specific medical and
historical setting. Although an incredibly versatile writer, he will,
however, probably always be best known for his creation of the hilarious
'Doctor' series.

Doctor on the Boil

Richard Gordon

HOUSE OF
STRATUS

This edition published in 2001 by House of Stratus, an imprint of Stratus Holdings plc, 24c Old Burlington Street, London, W1X 1RL, UK.

www.houseofstratus.com

Typeset, printed and bound by House of Stratus.

A catalogue record for this book is available from the British Library.

ISBN 1-84232-505-1

1

Across the main hall of St Swithin's Hospital, worn by generations of distinguished doctors and the patients who made them so, on a fine morning in early May two young men in short white jackets were ambling towards the plate-glass front doors.

'Why do you always do it in the spring, Terry?' asked Ken Kerrberry, the taller and more assured. 'It's so unoriginal. Just like getting flu in January.'

'But Ken, I tell you this time it's for real.' Terry Summerbee was dark-haired and wiry, with a ready smile.

'Let's recap, now. The spring before last you were really in love with that well-vatted physiotherapist who treated your strained quadriceps –'

'Could you blame anyone for going after a bird rhythmically massaging her way up your thigh to a tape of Strauss waltzes?'

'Last spring it was that little redhead in the refectory. At least she used to give you double helpings of chips. Well, what's this year's model look like?'

Terry hesitated. 'I don't want it to get round. There might be too much competition.'

'I swear professional secrecy, by the sphincter of Hippocrates.'

'What about you yourself?' Terry asked suspiciously.

'You know I'm already being drained of energy by that girl from TV –'

'All right. Mine's called Stella Gray. She's that new blonde one down in X-ray. Perhaps you've noticed her?'

'Noticed her? You might ask if I'd noticed Cleopatra turning up to take our see-through pictures. But my dear Terry –' He laid a fatherly hand on his companion's shoulder. 'I do implore you, forget it.'

'Oh? Trying to put me off? Then you *are* after her – '

'No, no! But she's right out of your class.'

'Thanks. A nice friendly remark.'

'You're right. It *is*. To start with, her father's a millionaire – '

'Yes, it's all round the hospital. He's in polymer resins, though don't ask me what anyone could possibly want them for.'

'She's jet set. We aren't even off the ground. She's been around – St Tropez, Nassau, Nepal. You name it, she's revelled in it. She won't look at mere medical students, I assure you. Even housemen and registrars are liable to get their fingers frozen.'

'I happen to know she's melting in my direction. As for the money, that doesn't make the slightest difference to me.'

'Personally, I can't understand what she's doing in a dump like this at all.'

'She has a sense of vocation and she's keen on photography.'

'You take my advice and leave her playing happily among the barium enemas.'

'I intend to ask her out,' Terry said firmly.

Ken laughed. 'That'll set you back. It's no good trying to fob her off with a bag of crisps and a trip up the Post Office Tower, you know. And don't forget, mate – the dean's little class examination in medicine strikes on Monday week. If you fail it's back six months, and no excuses. We won't be able to talk him round this time. You know what a mood the old dear has been in the last few weeks – twice as dithery and half as connable.'

'Relaxation is the best preparation for both childbirth and examinations,' Terry told him smugly.

They had reached the front doors, giving on to a broad flight of stone steps and the courtyard, in which some half-dozen grimy-looking plane trees were struggling into bud. The courtyard itself was separated from the road by a line of stout iron railings, pierced by gates flanked by two brick pillars. The pair watched with idle curiosity as a Rolls-Royce swung through the gates and came to a halt at the foot of the steps. Their feelings turned to surprise as the occupant got out, parking in that spot being strictly forbidden even for the dean. They turned to frank alarm with a better view of the driver. The two young men stood wide-eyed and open-mouthed as a tall, burly figure dressed outlandishly in a knickerbocker suit of gingerish tweed, on his head a deerstalker cap, on his face an aggressive beard, came stamping determinedly up the steps.

'It can't be!' Terry gasped. 'I never believed he really existed.'

'It's like meeting the griffin or some other fabubus beast,' exclaimed Ken.

'If you ask me, more likely the abominable snowman –'

'You! You two. You would be medical students, would you not?'

'Y–yes, sir.'

'I thought as much.'

Sir Lancelot Spratt, FRCS, stood stroking his beard, transfixing them with the glare that, until his retirement, had impaled generations of St Swithin's men with surgical efficiency.

'Are you familiar with the writings of the seventeenth-century English philosopher, Thomas Hobbes?'

'Not *intimately* familiar, sir,' said Ken, the braver of the two.

'He described the life of prehistoric man as poor, nasty, brutish, and short. I have always felt that an apt description of the modern medical student. Stand up, boy!' he roared. 'Take your hands out of your pockets. It is not only offensively unaesthetic, but it will give you osteoarthritis of the cervical vertebrae in middle age. What stage have you reached, in what you are pleased to call your education?'

'Second medical clerking, sir,' they said hastily together.

'H'm. Though I suppose you haven't much time for studies these days? Doubtless you occupy yourselves beating unfortunate policemen over the head with banners at demos. I abhor violence,' he told them forcefully. 'I know you're all hair and high principles, but if you happen to object to the state of the world you were born into, write letters to the newspapers. The pen is mightier than the sword. *That* is what civilization is all about, though I don't suppose it had occurred to you.'

'I'm a pacifist, sir,' said Terry.

'They always seem to get into bloodier fights than anyone else. Well, I can't waste all day with you.' Sir Lancelot strode into the building. 'Porter! Where's that blasted porter? Dozing as usual, I suppose?'

The head of Harry the porter appeared round the glass screen of his lodge. For a moment the man's expression suggested he saw St Peter himself, impatiently rattling his keys. But having kept his job for twenty years solely through the quickness of his wits, his gnarled face assumed a smile as he said, 'It's Sir Lancelot! What a surprise. I'm real pleased to see you again, sir.'

'You are *not* pleased to see me at all,' the surgeon informed him. 'You omitted to pay over my winnings from the very last bet I asked you to place for me, at Kempton Park on the afternoon I retired.'

'Did I, sir?' He looked aghast. 'It must have slipped my memory, being so upset at you leaving us – '

'Don't blather, man. Is the dean in?'

'His board says so, sir.'

'Good. Well, follow me. Jump to it. I never move about this place without an escort. And what are those trolleys doing hanging about in the main corridor? Get them tidied away immediately. The patients don't want to walk into the place and be reminded they might be pushed out of it.' His eye fell on a notice board. 'And kindly remove that Ministry poster saying, "We want Your Blood". Could easily be taken wrongly by nervous patients. Good grief, nurse – what's the laundry been doing to your uniform?'

A young blonde nurse stopped dead, regarding him with the same alarm as the two students.

'I can distinctly see your patellae,' he told her.

'Oh! Yes.' She looked down at her skirt. 'It's the new matron, sir. She's given us permission to shorten our uniforms. To be more fashionable, sir.'

'I imagined St Swithin's followed the dictates of Harley Street, not Carnaby Street,' Sir Lancelot told her loftily. He peered at the bib of her uniform. 'Is that what's wrong with you?'

She fingered the metal label. 'That's my name, sir. I'm Nurse Smallbones. We all wear them now.'

'Good grief,' muttered Sir Lancelot again. 'You wouldn't find *me* agreeing to that. I always preferred to do my duties here in complete anonymity. Please lengthen your clothes, nurse. They are quite immodest. Harry, where are you! I'm off to the dean.'

Rubbing his hands briskly together, as though making for a good dinner or an interesting operating list, Sir Lancelot started down the crowded main corridor like a tank through a cornfield.

The dean's office was on the ground floor of the medical school, to the far side of the hospital building. Sir Lancelot had reached only half-way, when he pulled up suddenly with a shout of, 'You!'

'Good morning, Sir Lancelot,' said a pleasant faced, curly-haired young man with a small fair moustache, in a long white coat with a stethoscope round his neck. 'I thought you were still living it up among the geishas? I do hope you had a good time? How was the Taj Mahal by moonlight?'

'I did not see the Taj Mahal, through indisposition. What the devil are you doing here, Grimsdyke? I thought the hospital had purged itself of you long ago.'

'I'm doing a locum, for a junior medical registrar who's on honeymoon.'

'H'm. Knowing you, it's a wonder you didn't offer to be your registrar's locum on the honeymoon, instead.'

'I don't think I'd have enjoyed it much, sir. The registrar's a she.'

'Oh…is a junior registrar job the best you can do for yourself? At your age?'

'Come, sir.' Grimsdyke pulled the end of his moustache, looking pained. 'I'm not that old. And these days the seven ages of man seem to be telescoped a bit. There's only youth and doddering senility.'

Sir Lancelot glared. 'And which category do I come into, pray? I'm genuinely disappointed you haven't climbed higher up the medical ladder. Even if the lower rungs are admittedly as crowded as Oxford Street during the sales – with the same ruthless elbowing going on, too. Not content with having been our oldest student, you want to be our oldest junior doctor. If your ambition's simply to become the Peter Pan of the medical profession, I suppose it's your affair.'

'I have other interests, sir,' Grimsdyke informed him.

'Medical moonlighting, eh? There's plenty of it about – struggling doctors working all week-end so that prosperous middle-aged ones can play golf. To be expected, I suppose, with the disgraceful rates of junior hospital pay.'

'I took this job as a refresher-course, really. One does get so terribly out-of-date. Now I know why I kept failing my finals – I was a student so long, all the treatment I was taught at the beginning had by then been discovered as highly dangerous.'

'Well, keep out of my hair, anyway.'

'But surely, sir, you've retired –'

'We'll see about that,' Sir Lancelot told him shortly. 'I mustn't keep the dean waiting any longer. I told the fellow I'd be here an hour ago.'

2

Dr Lionel Lychfield, Fellow of the Royal College of Physicians and dean of St Swithin's Medical School, was a little man with a bald pointed head, large pointed ears and a lined brow, resembling a short-tempered garden gnome. He was nervous and jumpy at the best of times, though inclined to be vague and forgetful – had he chosen to be a surgeon rather than a physician, much of the contents of his operating theatre would assuredly have finished up inside his patients. His awareness in the past week that Sir Lancelot was not only back in England but intending to call at St Swithin's had made him jumpier and shorter-tempered than ever. That morning, he could hardly bring himself to leave his house. But a letter waiting on his hospital desk put all thought of Sir Lancelot, or of anything else at all, clean out of his mind.

He sat on the edge of a high-backed leather chair in an office lined with mahogany cases of leather-bound books, decorated with busts of Plato and Lord Lister and a handsomely-framed reproduction of Luke Fildes' picture *The Doctor*. The letter which had so affected him lay alone on the blotter. The dean bounced gently, hands clasped tightly under his chin, staring fixedly at the handwriting and the torn envelope marked 'Strictly personal'. He read it yet again, with delight undimmed by familiarity.

It was addressed from the Garlick Club in St Martin's Lane, one of the most aloof in London. Its message was simply,

Dear Lionel,
Keep your nose clean!
Yours,
Willie.

'So it's all fixed!' The dean's eyes glowed behind his large round glasses. 'It just shows how useful it is, cultivating the right sort of friends in the right sort of places. Not *what* you know but *who* you know brings success. How alarming to think that applies even in medicine.'

He read it through again, as though the few words had some cryptic meaning so far eluding him. He drew a sheet of writing-paper from the rack, and pencilled on it, 'Sir Lionel Lychfield'. He looked at it admiringly, then added 'KBE'.

'Good morning, Sir Lionel,' he said to himself. 'How do you do, Sir Lionel? Your car is waiting, Sir Lionel. Is that Sir Lionel Lychfield speaking? Now students, three cheers for Sir Lionel...'

He added underneath, 'Lord Lychfield'. Feeling it looked elegant, he added, 'The Earl of Lychfield'. With a smile he went on, 'His Grace the Duke of Lychfield'.

'No knowing where these honours might stop, once one gets started,' he muttered, pencilling in 'HM King Lionel I.'

The door opened. 'Ah, Dean. Good to see you.'

The dean jumped up, cramming paper and letter as a ball into his jacket pocket.

'My...my dear Lancelot. I had quite forgotten you were coming.'

'Oh? You had my cable from New Delhi?'

'Yes, I'm sure I did... I'm afraid for the moment my mind was on other things. You see, I heard only this morning with much gratification that I am shortly to be –'

He stopped, horrified at his indiscretion. He was vague about the protocol, but he felt that leakage of the glad news would so upset Her Majesty the honour would automatically be cancelled. The word 'knighthood' had only to drop from his lips for his cup of happiness to be snatched away from them.

'I am shortly to be...to be...' he said unhappily.

'Good grief, you haven't put Josephine in the family way again at your age?'

The dean shook his head. 'To be given a free introductory lesson at a dancing school.'

'That hardly seems a cause for jubilation, I must say.'

'How was the Far East?' the dean went on hastily.

'Bloody.'

'Oh. Did you see the Taj Mahal by moonlight?'

'I did not see the Taj Mahal at all.' They both sat down. Crossing one knickerbockered leg over the other, Sir Lancelot observed, 'You've still got that ghastly sentimental picture by Fildes on the wall, I see. You know it was described by our late professional colleague and playwright James Bridie as depicting "a middle-aged man scratching his beard and wondering what the devil is the matter with a sick child he is expected to cure"?'

'I happen to like it.'

'I must say, Dean, I expected a rather more substantial welcoming committee. After all, I have been away from the hospital for some time.'

'Several members of the consultant staff have gone unexpectedly on holiday.'

'But they knew perfectly well I was coming.' The dean said nothing. 'That, I presume, is why they went unexpectedly on holiday? Well, I can only hope it keeps fine for them. Professor Bingham's here?'

The dean smiled. 'I don't think our new professor of surgery ever takes a holiday. Young and keen, you know. Bags of drive and energy. An excellent choice for the job.'

I bet that keenness is spilling a few basinsful of unnecessary blood, Sir Lancelot thought. But he said nothing. He was a fair man, who never made a professionally slighting remark behind others' backs. To their faces, of course, he allowed himself to be as colourfully offensive as possible.

'I gather from the newspapers you and young Bingham are in cahoots over this transplant business?'

'I am the physician, and he is the surgeon heading the team, certainly,' said the dean guardedly. 'A very good team, too. We have had some excellent results.'

'Yes, your last picture in the papers looked as though you'd just won the Cup Final.'

The dean looked offended. 'It is the surgery of the future.'

'In my old-fashioned view, we would be better employed trying to perfect the surgery of the past. My dear Dean! These surgical fashions – I've seen them come and go, like women's hats and skirts. Once we used to fill the patients up with liquid paraffin until they leaked. We tried to remove every organ compatible with the continuance of life, for every complaint from constipation to mother-fixation. After that, we invented the floating kidney, and lashed down everything inside the abdomen like deck-cargo in a storm. Do you remember the septic focus, Dean? I never saw one, quite honestly, but I seemed to have removed several hundred of the nasty little things. That was at the end of the war, when we thought they caused every bodily condition possible except pregnancy. Then we all forgot about them – I fancy because of the horrifying distraction of Nye Bevan with his National Health Service –'

'Where are you staying in London?' asked the dean. Sir Lancelot's reminiscences, though authoritative and captivating, quickly grew impregnable to interruption.

'I booked a room at the Crécy. I'll drive round later.' Sir Lancelot pulled a large red-and-white spotted handkerchief from his pocket and coughed into it.

'I only wish I could offer you hospitality. Josephine and I would be absolutely delighted if you could stay with us. Absolutely delighted! But we're quite full, right to the eaves. There's not only Miss MacNish, but now we've an *au pair* girl from Sweden, and the only spare bedroom the two children use for studying.'

Sir Lancelot grunted. 'How are your kids, anyway?'

The dean's expression, so far in the conversation resembling a man in the dentist's waiting for the drill to hit the nerve, relaxed into a proud smile. 'Muriel won the gold medal in anatomy, and George has got through his second MB – admittedly after one or two tries he is never at his best in examinations, being a somewhat nervous lad. So both have started work in our wards.'

The dean's fingers, feeling idly in his pocket, discovered a ball of crumpled paper. Mystified, he drew it out and spread it across the blotter. He read the message, hastily screwed it up and pocketed it again. 'To what must we be grateful for this – er, brief visit?' he asked Sir Lancelot, who was staring at him with raised eyebrows.

The surgeon helped himself to a pinch of snuff. 'I am here for two reasons. Firstly, I have a cough.'

10

'Oh? I'm sorry.'

'It's not frequent. Worse in the mornings. No haemoptysis, or anything sinister like that. It came on towards the end of my eastern tour. That's what prevented me from seeing the Taj Mahal – it seemed best not to risk the expedition, and anyway you can always look at the place on picture-postcards. I don't think I've anything serious. But of course, one must have any persistent cough investigated.'

'Most certainly.'

'So I've come to you. You're a member of the physicians' union. I'm a surgeon, and therefore know nothing whatever about the chest, except as a convenient shelf for your instruments while you're operating.'

'My dear Lancelot, of course I'll do what I can.' The dean was flooded with the sympathy of all medical men towards others undergoing the indignity of being ill themselves. 'Come up to my ward after lunch. I'll examine you and fix up X-rays and so forth, if necessary. There's a side-room empty at the moment, getting ready for the class examinations on Monday week.' He rubbed his hands. 'I'm really going to stretch the little blighters this time. There's been far too much slacking in the medical school lately, nothing but girls, poker, and electric guitars.'

'That's very good of you,' said Sir Lancelot amicably. 'My second reason is another complaint, one from which the whole world suffers. Boredom.'

The dean gave a sigh, drumming his fingers lightly on the desk. 'It is the blessing of our arduous profession, the unending flow of interesting work.'

'Exactly,' Sir Lancelot agreed firmly. 'As you know, I retired prematurely. At the height of my powers. But I felt I'd done my bit for both humanity and the tax-collector. I wanted to enjoy my country house in Wales. Perhaps it was selfish of me.'

'All of us here thought it an estimable idea,' the dean assured him warmly.

'Then of course my poor wife died. Now I'm lonely. One can fish only during the season. One cannot continually orbit the earth as a tourist. As an Englishman, I would not presume to interest myself in local politics, and anyway they are totally impossible to comprehend. I need an object in life.'

The dean nodded. 'They say philately can be most interesting. Or the collecting of butterflies and moths. Possibly bird-watching? Or pot-holing?'

'My dear Dean.' Sir Lancelot rose, with his hands behind his back, starting slowly to pace the room. 'You are of course familiar with the charter of our distinguished hospital?'

'Granted by Her Majesty Queen Elizabeth the First,' the dean recited fondly. 'I have often studied the original parchment. Quite awesome how its terms still govern much of our life here.'

'*Quite* awesome.' Sir Lancelot paused to cough. 'Then you will remember that the hospital's physicians and surgeons, though retired from active work, are fully entitled to return, to take over the care of such patients in the wards as they feel inclined to, with no questions asked. Clearly, our founders felt it desirable for the long experience of a retired surgeon never to be wasted –'

'Lancelot!' cried the dean.

'Of course, in those days people were always retiring to serve the Queen or explore the American colonies –'

'That right has never been exercised in the entire history of St Swithin's,' exclaimed the dean, turning pink.

Sir Lancelot fixed him with his eye. 'Well, it is now, old cock.'

'But...but...this is outrageous. Absolutely outrageous. What do you imagine in this day and age the patients would say? Supposing you walked into Professor Bingham's ward and simply told one of them that *you* were going to remove his gallbladder –'

'As my fees used to be the highest in London, they'd be getting better value for their National Health Insurance stamps.'

The dean slapped his desk-top. 'I shall have the charter amended.'

'That'll need an Act of Parliament. Ask the Prime Minister if you like, though there may possibly be more important things on his mind.'

'Really, Lancelot, this is most unreasonable of you,' the dean continued angrily. 'It'll raise all manner of problems with the Ministry. And just at the time I particularly want to keep my nose clean because –'

He stopped. 'Yes?' demanded Sir Lancelot.

'I happen to have mislaid my handkerchief. No, no, it'll never do.'

'We'll see about that. Meanwhile, I think I'll have a prowl round the old place. See you in the ward after lunch. And do provide a decent-sized jar for a specimen, there's a good chap. From some of the receptacles you physicians produce, you seem to imagine a camel could widdle through the eye of a needle.'

3

'Good grief,' muttered Sir Lancelot Spratt. 'Ruddy sacrilege.'

He felt a lump in his throat. A tear formed in the corner of his eye, ran down his rugged cheek and soaked into his beard. He dabbed it away with the red-and-white handkerchief and adjusted his features manfully.

'One mustn't mourn for bricks and mortar,' he told himself severely. 'But it's sad to lose the shrine of your memories.'

The cause of his distress was the surgical block of St Swithin's. It was never a handsome building. It had been erected about the time Lord Lister was introducing a lot of new-fangled nonsense called aseptic surgery, when architects believed institutions catering for the sick poor should have a forbiddingly ecclesiastical appearance, to put the patients in a pliable mood of terrified gratitude. It had resembled the cross between a Thames-side warehouse and Dr Arnold's thunderous chapel at Rugby School, but like so much of London's richness in Victorian curiosities it was no more. The wards Sir Lancelot once strode in surgical majesty had almost unbelievably vanished. So had the operating theatre in which he had won – and sometimes lost – so many bloody battles. Even the poky ill-lit lecture room, where he had hammered the finer points of surgery into the skulls of countless students, had been unsentimentally crushed to a heap of rubble. Now there was nothing left. Only a hole in the ground, with a bulldozer nosing up piles of mud and half a dozen men in white helmets drinking tea.

Sir Lancelot was about to revert from the harrowing sight when his eye caught something in the morning sunshine amid the brick fragments at his feet. He picked up a rusted scalpel – the old-fashioned sort with a fixed blade, the surgical equivalent of the cut-throat razor. He stroked his beard thoughtfully. 'I fancy that's the one I threw at my theatre sister during a nephrotomy in 1939,' he decided. 'Often wondered what became of it.'

He slipped the relic into the top pocket of his tweed jacket, and turning his back on the past made briskly for the new St Swithin's surgical block, which had risen on the site of the old kitchens and mortuary beyond the demolitions.

'Looks like a ruddy supermarket,' he grunted at the plate-glass-and-concrete tower. 'Strange, how in another hundred years that, too, will be thought a first-class eyesore. Though perhaps a medical supermarket's what's wanted,' he reflected. 'Push your little basket round the doctors, and complain like hell if the latest line of treatment isn't in stock. How different in my early days, when you didn't have to tell people what was wrong with them, you just told them what was good for them. *And* sent 'em away with a flea in their ear if they dared to ask any questions.' He sniffed as he entered the automatically sliding main doors. 'No smell. Nothing at all. I liked the old stink of antiseptic and stewing cabbage. It gave the place an atmosphere.'

He took the shiny staff lift to the top floor, where the professor of surgery had his wards. His intention was to see the sister in charge of the male patients, who on his own ward had for twenty years somehow tolerated his idiosyncrasies without even one attack of hysterics. He felt that she and Harry the porter, who had placed his bets and provided highly unreliable turf information over the same period, were the only people on the St Swithin's staff who interested him.

He walked along the short, plastic-tiled corridor frowning. The strangeness of modern wards was a shock to him, split into small rooms, hardly large enough to contain the surgical courtiers he liked following him. They were filled with the latest electronic equipment, which he cheerfully recognized he had no more hope of understanding than the latest pop singers' lyrics.

'Why, it's Sir Lancelot!'

Sister Virtue came fluttering joyfully towards him in her new-style uniform. It occurred to him that for the first time in his life he had seen the middle of her calves.

'My dear Sister.' He eyed her keenly. 'You're wearing make-up. On duty.'

'Oh! Yes. It's allowed now. The new matron, you know. In moderation, of course.'

He stroked his beard. Amazing, he thought. She didn't look such a bad old hag after all. 'A lot of things seem to be changing.'

She clasped her hands. 'Everything. The dean, the professor, the whole medical council, want us right up-to-date. All our equipment seems plastic and disposable – the syringes, the bedpans, the masks and gowns. I sometimes long for those lovely old chipped enamel washing bowls and the solid porcelain bottles.'

Sir Lancelot was inspecting the label on her uniform. 'In all these years you never told me that your name was Esmeralda.'

'Didn't I?' She blushed and looked at the floor.

'Pity. I rather like it.'

'Oh, Sir Lancelot!'

He smiled. He had always been aware of two weaknesses in his character – a tendency to go into an abdomen too easily, and a fondness for the ladies. Fortunately, he often told himself, he managed to keep both failings reasonably in check.

'Here, I say. It's Sir Lancelot. Sorry I wasn't at the door to greet you. Unbelievably busy these days, you know.'

The gallant conversation was interrupted by Professor Bingham himself, in a white coat and carrying a long ribbon of punched computer tape. Sir Lancelot did not gaze on his colleague affably. He had admittedly expressed the belief that Jimmy Bingham would end up as a professor of surgery when the young man was one of his own students. But he had hoped that the chair might be in Sydney, Vancouver or some other academic centre well away from St Swithin's.

'Morning, Bingham. A few innovations in the hospital, I see.'

'Even such a venerable institution as St Swithin's must recognize the progress of the twentieth century.' The professor pushed his glasses up the bridge of his nose, a habit which had irritated Sir Lancelot since he first interviewed the man for entry to the medical school. 'The adaptation has become a little easier with the retirement recently of so many older members of the consultant staff.'

'H'm,' said Sir Lancelot. The same attitude of mind, doubtless, he mused, enjoyed by Macbeth when he'd cleared away Duncan and Banquo. Well, if there's any haunting to be done, I've had a lifetime's experience in making flesh creep. He said nothing about the charter. It would be more amusing simply to snatch a patient or two and let Bingham work it out afterwards. 'What's that contraption in the corner?' he asked. 'Electrified bingo?'

Bingham's face took on a knowledgeable expression which Sir Lancelot found barely tolerable. 'That contraption, as you call it, is connected to the central computer. The days are passing when we had to examine patients with our bare hands, assemble the facts in our heads, and hit on a diagnosis. Quite out of date, like quill pens and inkpots. Now we do the requisite chemical investigations, feed them into the computer on punched tape, and within seconds receive the diagnosis. No possibility of error, to which all human beings are liable – even you, Sir Lancelot, eh?' Bingham smirked. 'In a few more years, of course, it'll be commonplace.'

'No need for dreary old flesh-and-blood doctors, you mean, except to sign sick notes and hold the vomit bowl? And what are you intending to do with that dirty great hole where the surgical block was, may I ask?'

Bingham's glasses seemed to flash with pride. 'That will be a new sterile unit entirely devoted to transplant surgery.'

'Good grief,' muttered Sir Lancelot.

'I take it you don't approve?' Bingham asked in a pained voice.

'I most certainly do not. The whole world's gone crazy about transplants. All sensationalism is deplorable, and in surgery it is unforgivable. Besides, it is all too experimental for *my* peace of mind.'

'You cannot turn back the advance of science,' said Bingham, shaking his head sagely.

'You take my advice and switch the money to something useful, like finding a cure for the common cold. Where's the cash coming from anyway? God knows, there's little enough of it about these days. The country can't even afford a regiment of Argylls and a decent motorway to Wales.'

'The dean handles all that. I cannot allow myself to be distracted by mere problems of finance. But we don't have to go begging to Whitehall.

The Blaydon Trust is supplying our funds, on, I understand, a generous scale.'

'The Blaydon Trust?' Something seemed to amuse Sir Lancelot. 'Well, well.'

'I gather Lord Blaydon is no longer alive, but the millions which he made from Ploughboy's Beer – which, being teetotaller even as a student, I regret that I have never tasted –'

'It's weasel's water,' observed Sir Lancelot. 'I suppose his widow controls the till? I once knew the lady socially.'

'We deal only with her lawyers. She appears to be a rather mysterious person. But she certainly seems to entertain an attachment to St Swithin's, for which we must be truly grateful.'

Sir Lancelot's eye fell on the patient in the nearest bed. 'What's the matter with that feller?'

A faintly shifty look came into Bingham's pink and chubby boyish face. 'He was admitted last night with abdominal pain and pyrexia.'

'What's the diagnosis?'

'I'm afraid the computer seems rather to have let us down. After all, we hadn't given it much to go on. But we shall be performing some twenty or thirty more tests on the patient this afternoon – punctures in various places for specimens of his body fluids, you understand – which doubtless will extract the answer.'

'Ask your computer if he's a Chinaman.'

'I beg your pardon?'

'Otherwise, to my old-fashioned bloodshot eye, he has the first faint tinge of jaundice. Good morning.'

Sir Lancelot stamped out of the ward. Hands in his jacket pockets, he stamped down the corridor to the lift. He pressed the button to descend then started to chuckle. Bingham was a fool, he reflected. Any man was, who imagined medicine a pure science when part of it was pure art, plus some witch doctoring and black magic. After two floors the lift stopped for a second passenger, who Sir Lancelot, lost in his thoughts, vaguely noticed as some member of the nursing staff.

'Ground floor all right?' he asked absently.

'Perfectly all right.'

He stood staring straight ahead at the lift doors. But something in those three words, an inflection in the voice, made a memory stir uneasily in its sleep. He pursed his lips. Slowly he changed the direction of his glance. 'Good God,' he muttered.

How fortunate I was in a hurry and took the lift. Usually I go down the stairs.'

'But what the hell are you still doing here?'

His companion smiled. 'And what the hell are *you* still doing here?' she asked pleasantly. 'I heard you'd retired.'

'I have, but – ' The significance of her uniform registered in his mind. 'Good grief, you're the matron.'

'Yes, except that nowadays it's known as the General Superintendent of Nursing and Ancillary Services. It's supposed to be more modern – or perhaps the idea is a grand title to compensate for the poor pay. And everyone still calls me the matron, anyway.'

Sir Lancelot leant to read the name pinned on her smart green uniform dress. 'Miss Charlotte Sinclair. Still? But what about that Mr Right you were going to marry?'

They reached the ground floor. The lift door opened to reveal the dean. 'Ah, Lancelot – '

'Sorry! Going up.' Sir Lancelot pressed the button for the top.

'Oh, I'd forgotten about *him*.' She laughed. The new St Swithin's matron was short and neat-limbed, fair-haired with green eyes and a turned-up nose. She was in her mid-thirties, but like all dainty women looked younger than she was. 'One can hardly marry the invisible man, can one?'

Sir Lancelot frowned. 'You left the hospital for that specific reason.'

'Surely you must have thought over the incident since, Lancelot? Why, you must be simpler than I suspected. That was the only way I could cool an ardour like yours.'

The lift stopped. The door flew back. Professor Bingham was waiting.

'Sorry,' snapped Sir Lancelot. 'Going down.' He pressed the button, complaining, 'Really, Tottie, you should have taken me more seriously. I was in love with you.'

'I know you were, dear Lancelot. But officially you were in love with your wife.'

'I think Maud would have given me my freedom. We were held together more by habit than affection. Like most couples, I suppose.'

'But what would your stuffy colleagues here have said?' The corners of Tottie's mouth creased, which had always excited him. 'The permissive society wasn't a going concern in those days, remember.'

The lift stopped. 'Lancelot, really –' complained the dean.

'Sorry, no room.' They shot upwards again. 'In those days? It was about the time of the Coronation, I recall. Then what did you do, Tottie?'

'I got a job in America instead. It was simple enough, with the shortage of nurses. I suppose I did pretty well, because I ended up running a hospital. Then last year I suddenly gave it up, to travel and see the country. Just before Christmas I made up my mind to come home.'

He shook his head slowly. 'It's like a dream now. Sorry Bingham.' He pressed the button.

'Did anyone find out about us in the end?'

'I've never had reason to suspect so. If you remember, Tottie, our affair was frustratingly discreet. Not to mention frustratingly pure. I think it was on Coronation night, in the corridor behind the old operating theatres, that you defended your honour with the left blade of a pair of obstetrical forceps.'

Tottie laughed. The lift halted. As the door slid open, Sir Lancelot shut it rapidly in the dean's face.

'That shows I'd more sense than is usually the case with a junior nurse,' she said as they went up again. 'Certainly more than the ones I'm in charge of today. Or did I? Perhaps the youngsters' outlook is right. They get more fun.'

'It's all comparative. We got excited simply holding hands in the back of the pictures. If I may say so, you're looking absolutely wonderful, Tottie.'

'Why, thank you. And you're exactly the same, you know.'

'I doubt that very much. Though I shall be hanging round the hospital for a while – which may give us a chance to find out.'

Bingham's angry face appeared briefly in the open lift door.

'And how is Lady Spratt?' Tottie asked, on their way down again.

'Didn't you hear?'

'Oh!' Tottie bit her finger. 'Yes, I remember now. I'm sorry.'

'No matter. I'm getting over it. However homespun the bonds, it's always a shock when they're sheared. Well, Tottie – '

The door opened. The dean put his foot in it. 'My dear Lancelot, has something gone amiss with the machinery? You've been going up and down like a yo-yo. I'm in a tearing hurry, too. Might I introduce you to our new matron?'

'How very kind,' beamed Sir Lancelot. 'By the way, Dean, we meet after lunch, don't forget.'

'Ah! Yes. 'Two o'clock. I'll get Bingham to remind me.'

Tottie made briskly off to her office. Sir Lancelot strolled thoughtfully past the site of the new building. It was remarkable. And perhaps a little exciting. He was going to enjoy his return to St Swithin's even more than he had imagined.

But first there was the dean at two o'clock, and Sir Lancelot remembered he had always had clammy hands and an ice-cold stethoscope.

4

When the bar in the students' common-room opened at five-thirty that evening, Ken Kerrberry said to Terry Summerbee, 'Look, there's that little thrombosed pile, George Lychfield. Do you suppose we could get out of him his father's questions for the class exam? Terry! You're not listening.'

'Sorry. I've a lot on my mind. Er – I'm revising my neurology.' When Ken repeated the suggestion, Terry shook his head. 'I shouldn't think the dean would confide in *him*.'

'But he might talk loudly in his sleep. Who knows? It's worth a try. George, you dear boy,' he called loudly. 'Let me buy you a drink.'

George's eyes lit up behind his large round glasses. He was a short, plump young man who resembled a garden gnome from the same mould as his father, if less weathered in appearance. Two related reasons made him accept the offer instantly. Firstly he could, like his father, never refuse anything free, from a drug firm's plastic golf-tees to an honorary degree. And his father's carefulness kept him even shorter of money than his contemporaries.

Ken bought him half a pint, mentioning idly, 'You know your revered father's putting the screws on the lot in my year next Monday week? I don't suppose he leaves the written questions hanging about the house, does he, so you might have a quick butcher's?'

George looked aghast. 'You must be joking? I could never do a dishonest thing like that. Not even if I was taking the exam myself.'

'But if by pure chance your eye *did* happen to fall upon the exam paper…' Ken took a gulp of beer. 'I'd give a *quid pro quo*, you understand. Anything you care to name.'

'Is that the time?' exclaimed Terry, staring at the wall clock.

'No, Ken,' George told him firmly, as Terry hastened for the door. 'There's nothing, absolutely nothing which could tempt me – ' He paused. 'Well…I hear you know a girl who works for TV?'

'Your suggestion is not only outrageous but highly insanitary.'

'No, no, I didn't mean *that*. I only had in mind an introduction. A professional introduction. You see – ' He looked round and dropped his voice. 'I wouldn't like this to get back to my father, but I've been writing a few scripts.'

'Not *more* hospital dramas – '

'No, quite different. Comedy scripts. They're really not bad. At least, our *au pair* girl thinks so, though she has a Swedish sense of humour, of course, and doesn't speak English very well.'

'I might possibly fix something,' Ken told him loftily. 'My bird works in the script department, too.' George's eyes shone brighter. 'But exam questions first. Intro after. All right?'

'All right,' George agreed in a guilty voice. 'Thanks for the beer. Sorry I haven't time to buy you the other half.'

Terry Summerbee was meanwhile hurrying down the flight of stone steps from the main hall to the X-ray department, which occupied a section of the basement, and like every other department in the Victorian building was so overcrowded with equipment as to appear in a permanent state of improvisation. Tightening the knot in his tie and looking round furtively for signs of the senior radiologist, he stepped determinedly among the apparatus towards a door at the far end marked DARK ROOM – KEEP OUT.

'Hello, there! Young Summerbee, I see. Brushing up your X-rays for the exam? Very keen of you. In my day, if I had the bad luck to be confronted with a radiograph I'd simply give a low whistle and say "That *does* look a nasty one". Surprising how often the examiner would agree heartily and let out what it was.'

Terry cursed under his breath. Dr Grimsdyke was popular among the students – as once the most experienced student in the country, he always saw their point of view. But he was inclined to be pushful, talkative, and a shade hearty – not at all the sort Terry wanted hanging about the scene of his delicate mission.

'I just thought I'd get a few films out of the X-ray museum.'

'Very wise of you. They always raid that little store of horror-pictures for the exams. But perhaps you'll allow me to point out that the museum's at the other end of the department?'

'Oh, is it?' asked Terry innocently. 'I don't know my way around as well as you do.'

'No, I think perhaps not,' agreed Grimsdyke. 'Toddle along now. If you find the baby who's swallowed a nappy-pin, notice its heart is pointing the wrong way. They caught me on that one way back in...well, the little thing is probably a father itself by now.'

Grimsdyke watched with a half-smile and Terry made towards the far end of the basement. When the student was safely through the door marked MUSEUM, he moved to the dark-room door and tapped on it.

'Come in. The light's on.'

Grimsdyke made his way through a double door guarding the entrance. The small room, with its open tanks and dripping fluids resembling some coastal grotto, was illuminated by the ghostly glow of diffuse light through negatives of human skeletons. Grimsdyke thought it lit rather prettily Stella the new pupil radiographer, with her long blonde hair falling to the shoulders of her white nylon overall – contrary to regulations, but she seemed to regard those as inconveniences only for other people.

'Any interesting snaps today?'

'You made that remark yesterday,' she said. 'Lover boy.'

'Did I?' Grimsdyke perched himself on the edge of a tank on the far side of the room. 'How about coming out tonight for a quiet dinner?'

'But lover man, I *told* you. It's my night for Oxfam.'

'Then how about tomorrow?'

'That's Thursday, isn't it? Oh... I've one of those boring evenings with my parents.'

'Then Friday?'

'Friday's the evening for my *cordon bleu* cookery classes, lover boy. And Saturday's booked for months and months.'

'Sunday?'

'Oh, I'm far too religious. Do you mind if I turn out the light?'

'No, no, go ahead.'

Illuminated only by a dull red glow from the corner, Stella started splashing in a tank. Grimsdyke rose and moved close to her.

'Lover, have you the letters MTF after your name?'

'What's that? Medical Technology Fellow, or something?'

'Must Touch Flesh. Honestly, you've got quite an obsession.'

Grimsdyke sat down again. There was a knock on the outside door.

'Come in, and mind the double doors,' she called.

He sat pulling his moustache in the darkness, annoyed at the intrusion of some other member of the X-ray staff. But a voice said, 'Stella...where are you?'

'Do you mind? You're touching me.'

'I was just feeling your face. You know, to recognize you. Like the blind,' said Terry Summerbee.

'All right, lover boy,' she said wearily. 'You know I've no warts and I'm female. Well?'

'How about coming out tonight?' Terry favoured the direct approach to all problems, in medicine and in life.

'But lover man, tonight's my *cordon bleu* cookery class.'

'Then tomorrow?'

'Parents, lover man. I'm dutiful, you know. They gave me life.'

'How about Saturday? I'm quite free.'

'Saturday I contemplate. About Sunday. When I fast all day in my bedroom. Sorry, lover boy.'

Terry swallowed. He decided to persist because Stella kept calling him lover boy. He was unaware that at the time she called everyone lover boy, even traffic-wardens and her father. 'Let's go through next week.'

'Listen, lover, if you really want to take me out, we could get it over and done with tomorrow.'

'But I thought tomorrow was your parents' home night, or something.'

'Did I say that? I must have touched on the wrong button.'

'See you in the courtyard when you get away at six, then?' Terry said eagerly.

'I'll be there, lover man. Be careful with the doors as you go out.'

Waiting until he heard the outer door firmly shut, Grimsdyke gave a guffaw. 'How sweet.'

' 'Terry's nice. Gentle, you know. Like a puppy.'

'Stella, my pearl shining in the darkness –'

'Take your hands off the jewellery. I'm turning on the lights.'

She started busily sorting dried X-ray pictures into large manila envelopes.

'But surely, Terry's not to be taken seriously?'

She gave a pout of her full lips. 'Why not?'

'He's not for *you*, Stella. You need a man of the world to take you around. A man of experience.'

'Are you trying to pull the generation gap, or something, lover man? That's new.'

'Anyway, you can't go out with him tomorrow. You promised to go out with me.'

'Did I?' She went on sorting the X-rays. 'I must have flipped the wrong switch.'

'I'll be there, anyway. Six, at the front door.'

'As you wish, lover, as you wish,' she said accommodatingly.

'I'm very, very tender towards you, Stella.' Grimsdyke put his arms round her from behind and started gently biting her neck. 'Like it?'

'Hardly preferable to mosquitoes.'

'How about a nice –'

'Gaston, lover man, take this packet of X-rays to the dean's office, will you? He wanted them specially.'

'Oh, all right,' said Grimsdyke disconsolately. 'But tomorrow, at six. Lover girl.'

5

The dean usually reached home at seven. He parked his Jaguar that evening in the mews garage of his house, and carrying his document-case opened the back door with the pleasurable sensation of a man going to break good news, particularly when it is about himself. He hung his homburg in the hall, and with jaunty step opened the door of his small ground floor study. His smile vanished as he found it occupied by his son George.

'What are you doing rummaging in my desk?'

'Oh! Hello, Dad. I was looking for this week's *B.M.J.*'

'Since when have you been so anxious to keep up with the latest medical discoveries? You have quite enough to tax your mind learning those of the past five centuries.' The dean's eyes narrowed. 'You weren't searching for the class examination questions, I suppose?'

'Me, Dad? But I'm not even taking the exam.'

'Precisely. But I wouldn't put it past some of the other students to bribe you.'

'Dad! What a shocking thing to say.'

'It is, but that doesn't make it any less likely. There are some quite disreputable characters in the medical school these days. And you must choose your friends more carefully, now that I'm to be made—' He stopped. 'Maid of all work, young Inga,' he remarked as the *au pair's* blonde hair appeared round the door. 'Will you ask my wife to come here a moment?' he added. 'Now go up to your room, George, and open your books. The life of a medical student contains not a single minute to be wasted. You might quite easily learn something of considerable importance before dinner.'

'Dad –' George shifted his feet. 'I wonder if I'm really suited for medicine.'

'Of course you are,' his father told him briefly. 'We've had medical men in this family since the days of Gladstone bags and leeches. I wish you'd follow the example of your sister. *She* will certainly be studying upstairs with her usual diligence. And what, might I ask, would you intend to do instead?'

'I've thought of the – er, drama.'

The dean snorted. 'Just because you make a fool of yourself in the hospital pantomime, you seem to imagine you're a combination of Bernard Shaw and Brian Rix.'

'But everyone says I've got talent.'

'Who does? Inga, I suppose? And don't you go fiddling about with her, either. I've noticed it. We maintain certain standards in this family, even if the rest of the country is nothing but pot, pill, and pornography. Ah, there you are, my dear.'

George made his escape. His mother was a tall, good-looking, and smartly dressed woman, with kind grey eyes and a soft nature, which to the dean had the comfortable attraction of a fireside sofa on a chilly afternoon. He unlocked a cupboard in the corner and produced a decanter of sherry.

'Josephine, let us drink a toast.' He poured two glasses. 'To...no, let's make it to *you*. To the future Lady Lychfield.'

She stared at him. 'It's all fixed,' he added with a wink. 'I had a letter from Willie at the Ministry. Wheels have been turning. My years of unselfish service to St Swithin's and medicine in general are to have their just reward, on the Queen's birthday to be exact. Though now I come to think of it,' he added, 'they ought to have given me a knighthood years ago.'

'Oh, Lionel!' she gasped. '*Sir* Lionel.'

The dean kissed her lightly on the cheek. 'Makes it worthwhile being married to me all these years, eh?'

Her eyes glowed. He thought he had never seen her looking so beautiful. How strange – in a country where even prime ministers take pains to make known they put the same bottled sauce on their chips as the rest of the population – is the feudal potency of the twice-yearly honours list.

'Though not a word to a soul,' he told her sternly. 'Of course, I've got to keep my nose clean for the next month or so, as Willie says, but that's hardly an obstacle. Knight Commander of the Most Excellent Order of the British Empire.' The words rolling round his mouth were more intoxicating than the sherry. 'Though naturally, I don't give tuppence for titles and suchlike myself,' he added quickly. 'I'll accept it only as an honour to the hospital. It's high time we had a knight again on the staff of St Swithin's –'

He paused. A cloud had drifted across the sunshine of his life. 'I'd forgotten. Sir Lancelot.'

'He's dead?' she exclaimed.

'No damn fear. That man's as indestructible as a fossilized rhinoceros. He's back from the Far East.'

'How splendid! We must ask him to dinner.'

'There's no hurry.' Toleration of Sir Lancelot he thought one of those items in any woman's life quite beyond the understanding of her husband. 'He's going to stay in London quite a while. But most certainly not with us.'

The dean stared through the window, where dusk was falling over the pleasant, neat green circle of Regent's Park. His house was large, but near Harley Street and the West End, affording a precious feeling of spaciousness amidst the dignified crescents and tree-lined streets spreading towards the northern slope of London.

'Perhaps he'll quarrel with everyone and go back to Wales,' the dean consoled himself. 'He only resigned from the staff because of a row with the last professor of surgery.' Whether this was over the higher principles of operative technique, or because the professor insisted on parking his Mini in the corner of the courtyard reserved by tradition for Sir Lancelot's Rolls, no one at St Swithin's ever found out. 'Though it's annoying. An old curmudgeon like him could easily upset all the exciting changes we're seeing at St Swithin's.'

'If the fishing season's open, he may not stay a long time, dear.'

'Any time is long in the company of Lancelot,' he said wearily.

There was a knock on the study door. It was Miss MacNish, the cook-housekeeper, a pleasant, neat, competent, red-headed Aberdonian in her thirties, who they had snatched eagerly from Sir Lancelot's service on his leaving London.

'Sir Lancelot Spratt is back in London,' the dean informed her sombrely.

'Now isn't that good news, Doctor! Have you invited him to stay?'

'I have *not* invited him to stay.'

'I'll bake him one of those Dundee cakes he enjoys so much. It'll be a nice change after all that curry and chop suey he must have been getting. I came to say your dinner's ready.'

The dean shook his head. Women were quite ridiculous when it came to judging a man's character. No wonder so many of them ended up in the divorce courts. He reached the door before he remembered Sir Lancelot's X-rays. He turned back to open his document case. He held the pictures up to the reading-lamp. He gasped.

'Oh, no!' The film shook in his hand. 'It can't be?' He stared more closely. 'Dear me! But it is. Poor fellow. Poor Lancelot. To think that I could have spoken so harshly of the dear, unfortunate man.'

6

'Officer,' demanded Sir Lancelot from the window of his Rolls. 'I would appear to have lost a hotel. Perhaps you'd kindly direct me to the Crécy?'

'But it's right opposite, sir. The tall white building.'

A frown congealed on Sir Lancelot's broad forehead. '*That* overgrown silo?'

'Maybe you're thinking of the old hotel, sir? That was pulled down.'

'Good grief. They haven't pulled down Buckingham Palace yet, I suppose?'

The policeman grinned. 'No, sir. But from what they're charging at that little pub opposite, you might find staying at Buckingham Palace a bit cheaper.'

Sir Lancelot drove into the hotel forecourt, which to his puzzlement was crowded with young and noisy females.

'Some sort of demo, I suppose,' he decided, slamming the car door. 'Or a carnival. Though I suppose today they wear those sort of clothes even at funerals.' His face lit as he recognized the same manager standing in black jacket and striped trousers beside the doorman. 'Luigi! How good to see you. Though your establishment has undergone a somewhat alarming metamorphosis.'

'A pleasure to have you staying again, sir.' The tall, white-haired Italian was a dignified figure suggesting a particularly experienced doyen of the diplomatic corps in some stylish capital. 'I'm afraid the days of the old-fashioned family hotel in London are over. But I assure you our comfort and service are maintained. We have put you on the sixteenth floor, next to the Picardy suite. And the chicken *à la kiev* in the grill-room is as good as ever.'

'Is Potter-Phipps still your hotel doctor?'

'Alas, no. We have a new man – quite young, and very brilliant, so he leads me to understand. The doorman will garage your car,' he added, as the porter collected Sir Lancelot's suitcases.

'Kind of you to come and greet me in person, Luigi.'

The manager looked a shade uncomfortable. 'I have in fact another guest due any moment. One as important as yourself Sir Lancelot. Eric Cavendish. You know, the film actor.'

'Is *he* still going? I'm sure I used to see him in a double-bill with the new Buster Keaton.'

The manager laughed. 'He is as popular as ever – with the teenagers particularly, as you can see.'

'Odd,' murmured the surgeon. 'I suppose Freud has the answer, if I could ever understand what the fellow is talking about.'

As he spoke, screaming broke out in the crowd. Luigi hurried forward as a chauffeur-driven Mercedes drew up. The manager shepherded into the hotel a tall slim man followed by a short fat one, both wearing large dark glasses despite night having fallen.

'I suppose he's in the Picardy suite?' Sir Lancelot asked the porter. 'I'll let the fuss die down before I venture up, I fancy. Besides, I've had a long day driving from Wales and am in need of the bar, if you still have such old-fashioned nooks among all this functional plastic.' He stopped in the hotel doorway. 'Piped music! The country's getting like Prospero's isle – *"Sometimes a thousand twanging instruments Will hum about mine ears; and sometimes voices..."* and I don't bloody well like it.'

The first action of Eric Cavendish on reaching the Picardy suite was to remove his toupee, which was itching. Then he took off his dark glasses and with care inspected his eyelids for puffiness. Next, he opened a small crocodile-skin hand-case full of plastic containers, and selecting one green pill, one blue, two orange, and another with red and yellow stripes on it, went to the bathroom for a glass of water and swallowed them.

'That's better, Ted,' he announced to the fat man, his British agent who had met the plane from New York. 'God, it's great to be back in dear old

London Town! The place where I was born, you know. You might call me a citizen of the world – I've an apartment in Paris and a production company in Hollywood, I've been married in Las Vegas and divorced in Mexico, I've my bank account in Switzerland and I pay my taxes in Liechtenstein – but I only feel at home here, right here.'

Ted, who had kept his glasses on, asked, 'Have you any plans for tonight, Eric? The wife and I thought maybe a quiet dinner after your trip –'

'My plans are very beautiful.' He looked at his watch. 'In ninety minutes the most wonderful little dolly in the world is going to come through that door. I'm entertaining her up here for dinner – just the two of us, quiet after the trip, as you said.'

Eyebrows rising above the dark glasses indicated Ted's interest. 'Do you suppose I'd know her?'

'No.' Eric started undressing for a shower. 'I met her on my TV show in New York. She was over on some sales-promotion trip – Miss Toothpaste or Miss Garbage-cans, or something spine-chilling like that. I made a date. I called her up this morning before take off. And it's all go.'

'Where's she live?'

'Let me see – I've forgotten the geography of this town. Place called Tooting. Quaint name, eh?' The actor laughed. 'I guess it's historical. Fashionable?'

'It's had a lot of improvement schemes recently,' Ted said evasively. He lit a cigarette. 'How old is she?'

'Seventeen.'

There was a short silence. 'Look, Eric – I don't see so much of you these days, but I was your mate as well as your agent back when you started. So I can talk in a brotherly way. Right? Why don't you ease up?'

'Why?' asked Eric Cavendish gaily, pulling off his shirt and starting to unzip his stays. 'I like 'em that age, and they like me.' He paused. 'Did I remember to take the striped pill?'

'That's what I mean. I'm worried about your health. You were pretty sick that time in California.'

'And do you know how I pulled through? I had an English doctor and an English nurse. They were terrific. I remember one night I just wanted to turn it all in – curl up and die, never look another day in the face again. But that nurse, she sat just holding my hand like a kid and talking to me. I guess she saved my life.'

'If you need a doctor now, there's one attached to the hotel. I took care to find out.'

'Thanks, Ted. But I've never felt fitter. Nor younger. Do you mind if I ask you to leave? I've got my electric massage, then my medicated bath and my meditation.'

An hour and a half later, Miss Iris Fowler of Tooting Bec, the reigning Miss Business Furnishing, was calmly asking at the porter's desk for Mr Eric Cavendish.

'Yes, he's expecting you, Miss. The page will show you up.'

She was a short blonde girl with delicate, babyish features and large long-lashed blue eyes, wearing a dress which Sir Lancelot would have described as wholly suprapubic. In the lift she took a deep breath.

She was not particularly looking forward to the evening. There were a dozen boys of her own age she would have preferred to spend it with. But she was a clear-headed girl. She wanted to break into modelling or television or the films – anything to get free from a typewriter. Being Miss Office Furnishing, to her disappointment, seemed to lead nowhere. But an hour or so alone with Eric Cavendish might achieve a lot.

'Hello, there,' the actor greeted her enthusiastically. His toupee was securely fixed, his eye-lotion applied, his girdle tightly zipped, his skin massaged and medicated, his mind heightened by meditation. 'And how's my baby doll?'

'Very well, thank you, I'm sure.'

He laughed. 'That sweet British accent! I'm British, you know. At least, I started off that way. I was taken to the States when I was a kid.'

'Well, fancy that.'

'Have you seen all my movies?'

'Oh, yes.'

'You liked them?'

'Yes, ever so.' She added, 'Thank you,' being a carefully brought-up girl.

Eric poured the martinis. Dinner was served and eaten. He talked about himself while she looked at him with her big soft eyes, and he thought her a delightful conversationalist. When the meal was cleared away and the waiters handsomely tipped, he sat next to her on the sofa and decided to get on with things.

'Quite a place to visit, London these days.'

'Oh, yes. There's the Tower, the Changing of the Guard—'

'I mean for sex.'

'Oh, sex. Yes. I suppose so.'

'If you want to do it, you just do it.'

'Do what?'

'Sex.'

Her eyes fell on the electric wall clock. 'Oo, is that the time? I've got to think of my last bus.'

He laughed. 'You go on a *bus?* There's democracy or socialism or whatever you label it. Let's take our time. I'll hire you a car.'

'No, I mustn't be late. My dad will worry that I've had an accident.'

'Shall we get on with it, then?'

She swallowed. 'All right. Thank you.'

He led her into the bedroom, murmuring, 'Do you mind if I put out the light? I'm strangely shy.'

'Please yourself, do.'

In the dark he removed his suit, his girdle, and the copper band he wore against rheumatism. 'Where are you, baby doll?'

'I'm on the bed. It ain't half cold.'

'I'll be with you...' He took off the rest of his clothes, to enjoy it the more. Arms outstretched, starting to breathe heavily, he stumbled through the darkness. 'Here I am, baby doll.'

He climbed on to the bed. 'Coo, you *are* hairy.' She giggled. 'It tickles.'

'Where are your lips?' he asked throatily. His sexual technique, like his acting, had through experience become automatic, though it was polished, if a little old-fashioned, and generally satisfied the audience.

'Oh, sorry,' she apologized. 'I was looking the other way.'

'I'm going to bite you.'

'Will you do it where it doesn't show? The girls in the office—'

'Or maybe you just want me to go ahead?'

'Well, there's no point in wasting time, is there?'

He gave a soft laugh. 'You London girls! Eager!'

'I've still got to think of my bus –'

He gave a loud cry. She sat bolt upright. 'What's the matter?'

'It's gone again!'

'What's gone?'

He gasped. 'I'm going to die.'

'Blimey.'

'Put on the light.'

'I don't know where it is.'

'Beside the bed, you damn fool.'

She fumbled for the switch. He was sprawled face-down, groaning and holding the small of his back.

'Fetch a doctor.'

'I got my first-aid badge in the Guides –'

'A doctor! Ring down to the desk.'

'I don't want nobody to see me like this,' she told him spiritedly.

'There's a bath-robe...in the closet...'

'This never happens in any of your films,' she complained.

'Please! Get a doctor. I implore you.'

She screamed loudly.

'What in God's name –'

'Your head!' she cried in horror. 'The top's coming off.'

He replaced his toupee. 'Get a doctor, there's a good little girl. A doctor! I'll do anything for you, anything...'

Her eyes lit up. 'My mum says I deserve a modelling career –'

'All right, all right, I'll fix it. For both of you. But for God's sake get the doc before it's too late. And cover me up with something before I catch pneumonia as well.'

The doctor was quickly found in the grill, where he was finishing dinner at the hotel's expense. He hurried from the lift to the Picardy suite, his mind already busy with the case – the suite was invariably taken by rich, elderly overseas visitors, and he was calculating what the latest occupant would stand in the way of fees. To his surprise, the door was opened by a young girl in a man's short dressing-gown.

'Good evening. I'm Dr Grimsdyke. Are you the patient?'

'No, there's a gentleman took queer suddenly in bed.'

'Oh, what a shame,' said Grimsdyke sympathetically. 'Well, I'd better have a look at the fellow, hadn't I.'

He recognized the actor at once. 'Eric Cavendish! I've always wanted to meet you. But why do you happen to be lying under that candlewick bathmat?'

'My back,' he groaned. 'It's gone again.'

Grimsdyke assumed a professional manner. 'Were you putting any strain on the back?'

'What the hell do you suppose I was doing with that dolly? Mind-reading?'

'Ah, the old love-muscles sometimes let us down,' Grimsdyke told him gravely. He poked with his finger. 'Hurt?'

Eric Cavendish let out a cry.

'I think we'd better apply traction, if the young lady can help. What's her name?'

'I've forgotten,' said the patient distractedly. 'But she's Miss...Hardware, or something.'

Iris' head appeared round the door from the sitting-room. 'If you wouldn't mind, I'd like my clothes.'

'Miss Hardware, would you kindly take the patient's arms while I pull his feet?' There was a thunderous knocking on the outside door of the suite. 'Perhaps you'd better answer that first,' Grimsdyke told her. 'I'll give a few preliminary tugs. Tell me if I hurt.'

Eric Cavendish gave another loud howl.

'Grimsdyke!' It was Sir Lancelot in a tartan dressing-gown. 'I might have thought as much. How the devil do you expect me to get a minute's sleep when the place sounds like Dante's Inferno? What are you organizing in here? Some sort of sadistic orgy?'

'Good evening, Sir Lancelot. Case of acute lumbago. Perhaps you'd care to assist me?'

Sir Lancelot glared at Iris. 'I take it you're the patient's young daughter?'

'I am *not*! If you want to know, I'm just on my way to catch a bus.'

She snatched up her clothes and made for the next room. Sir Lancelot scratched his beard. 'I fear that I have perhaps been living in the country too long. I suppose you realize, Grimsdyke, that your treatment is all wrong? As I'm here, you'd better let me have a dekko. Don't worry, my good sir,' he said to the patient. 'I happen to be a consultant surgeon. I well remember how I was called to the old Duke of Skye and Lewis in similar circumstances. Not only had he fractured his ankle, but I had to invoke the services of a carpenter to free him from the wreckage of his own four-poster.' Sir Lancelot chuckled fondly. 'The dear old Duke was always a man of considerable ingenuity and enterprise.'

7

'My dear, dear Lancelot,' said the dean of St. Swithin's. 'My dear fellow! Little did I think – in all the years I have enjoyed your friendship – that I should have to break such terrible news to you. Well, you've taken it like a man. Not that I should have expected anything different from one of your character.'

Sir Lancelot gloomily dropped the X-ray picture on to the desk. It was late the following afternoon, and the pair of them sat alone in the dean's office.

'I should never have gone on that blasted tour of the Far East,' Sir Lancelot said resignedly.

'It is, of course, an extremely rare Asiatic disease you have contracted.'

'*That's* not much ruddy consolation.' The surgeon squared his shoulders. 'But I'm fine in myself. I don't remember being fitter. Despite a very poor night, I feel up to swimming the length of the Serpentine and then running right round Hyde Park. It's ridiculous.'

The dean sighed unhappily. 'That's the tragic part of it. Perhaps you are not altogether familiar with the symptomatology? I confess I had to look it up myself. According to the books, the patient has a euphoric feeling of well-being. It's a very marked feature of the condition. Until quite suddenly...woomph.'

'Woomph?' Sir Lancelot stroked his beard. 'How long? Twelve months?'

'Well...'

'Nine?'

'I'd say six.'

He nodded slowly. 'So I am to leave this polluted planet? Well, I've had a good life, I suppose. It comes to us all. And despite our own unshakeable inner conviction, the world will spin on as busily and just as happily without us.'

'You have given so much to mankind.'

'I don't know, but I've certainly taken a good deal out of it.'

The dean fiddled with the stethoscope lying on his desk. 'If you have any wishes – any last requests...?'

'Only one,' Sir Lancelot said in a firm voice. 'You may recall that yesterday I mentioned taking over some cases in the wards again, under the provisions of our founding charter. I don't fancy you took kindly to the idea.'

'Forgive me.' The dean was horrified at himself. 'I was being selfish, quite beastly selfish.'

'Let us overlook that,' Sir Lancelot told him handsomely. 'But I'd like to see a few patients now and then, in such time as I have left. After all, I've often been called a surgical carthorse. I might as well die in harness.'

'Any patients you like,' the dean invited generously. 'I'm sure they'll give their permission. Indeed, they'll be deeply grateful. They'll show their incisions proudly to their grandchildren, and say, "Sir Lancelot Spratt did that". Like war-wounds.'

'Quite,' said Sir Lancelot. He produced his spotted handkerchief and coughed gently.

'I'm sure Professor Bingham will open his surgical wards to you. He'll be doing his list in the theatre now. Why not put the idea to him?'

'I have one other small request. I am really rather uncomfortable in my hotel. The place is terribly noisy at night, everyone having sex orgies into the small hours – '

'Of course, you must move in with us.'

'I am touched, most touched – '

'With an open heart, we shall do all we can to make your last days happy.'

'I shall disappear to Wales to...for the...finally.'

The dean hesitated, and added generously, 'You may have my electric blanket.'

Sir Lancelot rose. 'Let's say, Monday week? I am already booked in the hotel till then, and I will have a lot of telephoning of solicitors and suchlike to put my affairs in order. Now I'll go and see Bingham.'

He added sombrely, 'He knows?'

'He knows.'

Sir Lancelot left the dean's office. He walked slowly into the open, past the hole in the ground to be filled with the new transplant unit. 'There's one advantage,' he muttered to himself. 'I shall never have to set eyes on *that* monstrosity.'

With gaze downcast, he entered the automatic doors of the new surgical block and took the lift for the top floor. A glance from the anaesthetic-room showed that Bingham was still operating, finishing the minor cases at the end of the list. With movements so familiar, Sir Lancelot took surgical gown, cap and mask from their containers. Visiting an operating theatre in a social way, he did not feel inclined to change his tweed trousers for something more sterile. His technique on these calls was to edge quietly to the operating table, inspect the surgeon's work for some moments unseen, then make his presence known with a sniff of disapproval which could be heard all over the theatre.

'It's Sir Lancelot.' Bingham looked up. 'Nurse – push my glasses up my nose, they've slipped again.'

'I suppose you realize you're doing that all wrong?'

'Am I?'

'You're cutting the gut before you've tied off the artery.'

'As intended. It's the new technique.'

Sir Lancelot snorted behind his mask. 'Sounds as if a damn fool invented it.'

'*I* invented it.'

'There you are, then – ' He paused. 'Forgive me, dear boy. As usual, I let my tongue run away with me. I am stupidly blind to the recent advances in surgery, which will carry our profession forward long after I myself am dead and gone.'

Bingham looked up again. 'I say, that's very civil of you.'

'In my time I have not perhaps done all possible to smooth the brief lives of those about me, nor taken account of the little failings which mark us all as human beings. I much regret it now. Sister, I believe you were a junior theatre nurse in my own active days?'

'That's quite right, sir.'

'I may have given you the rough edge of my tongue now and again?'

'You did once compare me to a chimpanzee with ten thumbs, sir.'

'I am sorry, deeply sorry.'

'You finish that,' Bingham directed his assistant, making for the surgeons' room and peeling off his gloves.

'You know I am not much longer for this unruly world, Bingham?' said Sir Lancelot, following him.

'I was very upset. As one of your students—'

Sir Lancelot held up a hand. 'If only more of them had possessed your intelligence, your energy, your endlessly questioning brain! I'm sorry if at the time I thought you something of a small-minded, conceited little prig.'

Bingham started stripping his gown. 'I wonder if I might ask a favour, Sir Lancelot? I'm sure you'll agree you're an exceptional man? Physically as well as mentally.'

Sir Lancelot inclined his head graciously.

'You know I'm head of the St Swithin's transplant team. So I wondered if, in I believe six months—'

'But I've got this filthy Asiatic disease,' Sir Lancelot objected.

'But parts of you are excellent. You're quite a curate's egg, one might say.' Bingham gave a laugh, hastily stifling it. 'Coming to the point, could I put a couple of my patients on the list for your kidneys?'

After a moment's hesitation, Sir Lancelot said gravely, 'It is only fitting that I should use my remains as I have used my life. To benefit suffering humanity.'

'I must say, that's a jolly good spirit. Fine. I'll get my secretary to make a note of it. And while we're on the subject, could we have your corneas?'

'Yes. I agree.'

'How about your heart?'

'If you can make as good use of it as I have.'

'Splendid. Are you planning to – er, end up in St Swithin's? It would save a lot of those difficult transport problems.'

'My dear Bingham, I cannot make detailed plans for the location of the event. I am going to perish, not have a bleeding baby.'

'Of course. Now, then. Liver?'

'As you wish.'

'Spleen? Pancreas?'

'You may.'

'Thyroid gland? Bone marrow?'

'Take the lot.'

'I've just remembered something. We owe High Cross Hospital a kidney, which they swapped for a pair of lungs. If you could help us out –'

Sir Lancelot drew himself up. 'I may, as you say, be exceptional. But not so exceptional as to possess three blasted kidneys. Now if you will excuse me, I shall take your surgical shopping list out to the West End and provide it with a damn good dinner.'

8

Sir Lancelot left the surgical block and paced, deep in thought, down the long main corridor of the old building towards the hall. As he reached the front door he became aware of a dark uniform blocking his path. Looking up, he saw Harry the porter.

'Might I have a word with you, sir?'

Sir Lancelot grunted.

Harry gave a nervous jerk of the head towards his cubicle. 'In private, like?'

'Are you suggesting I squeeze with you into that rabbit-hutch?'

Harry produced from inside his jacket a thick bundle of five-pound notes. 'It's about that little bet you mentioned yesterday, sir. The one what I put on for you at Kempton Park the very day of your retirement. I'm very sorry, sir, that I overlooked sending on your winnings.'

'Overlooked! Do you expect me to believe it was merely something which slipped what you care to call your mind? Rubbish, man. You're as crooked as an aberrant appendix. You've never overlooked the chance to swindle someone out of a ha'penny in your life. You'd con the rawest new student to buy a load of old instruments you'd probably pinched anyway, and you'd pawn the Chairman of Governors' overcoat if you thought you could get away with it. God knows what a scoundrel like you is doing in the employment of a respectable institution like St Swithin's. Personally, I wouldn't trust you to punch the tickets on a travelling Chinese brothel —'

Sir Lancelot stopped. He raised his hand to his eyes. The reference to the East exploded a bomb in his mind.

'My dear good man,' he continued gently. 'I was wrong, very wrong to get so cross. We all have our faults. What are yours, compared with the majestic tide of life and death, which sweeps away all traces of us from the sands of time? Pray, keep the money.'

Harry stared at him, half of his brain wondering if Sir Lancelot had gone mad, the other half trying to make out what the catch was.

'It is mere paper, of no importance.' Sir Lancelot pushed the man's hand aside. 'Put it to some good use. How little to pay for the pleasure your cheerful face has given me, every morning I arrived in the hospital, sticking from that hole thing in your cubicle. Good-bye, Harry. May you prosper. And *do* get out of that stupid habit of always backing the second favourite.'

As he turned away, pausing in the doorway to find his handkerchief and give a cough, he heard a female voice call his name.

'Why, it's the matron – ' He came back to the hall, giving a brave smile, 'And what can I do for you?'

'I'm so glad I caught you. It's about Nurse Smallbones.' Sir Lancelot frowned in puzzlement. 'You may remember, when you arrived in the hospital yesterday you seemed to find her skirt too short.'

'I most certainly did,' he said warmly. 'If our young ladies walk the streets of London off-duty displaying their erotogenic zones by the acre, that is perfectly all right by me. But when they're in St Swithin's they're nurses, *not* the star turns of striptease establishments.'

'I do hope Nurse Smallbones will meet with your approval now.' The girl was standing sheepishly behind her. 'She has lengthened her skirt right down to her ankles.'

'Exactly.' He nodded briskly. 'The nurses wore dresses like that in my young days, and I really saw no necessity to change them. The patients in our wards want – for once in their ruddy lives – to savour the tenderness of womanhood, not the sexiness. No female would ever wear a skirt above her calves out East – '

He stopped. He covered his eyes again. 'My dear girl,' he continued weakly to Nurse Smallbones. 'Please wear your dress any length you fancy. Serve the patients' dinners stark naked if the idea possesses you. Though I fear you would find our antiquated wards somewhat on the chilly side.

What does it matter if your clothes reach to your malleoli or your symphysis pubis? It is fashion, mere triviality, we spend our brief lives foolishly obsessed with such things. Back to your duties, Nurse Smallbones. And bless you, my child.'

'Are you feeling all right, Lancelot?' asked Tottie Sinclair in a puzzled voice.

'Yes. That's the saddest part of it.' Sir Lancelot bravely jutted his bearded chin. 'I have but six months left.'

'No!'

'The dean has just made the diagnosis. A physician of his calibre can hardly be imagined to make any mistake.'

'But...but what is it?'

'An obscure Asian disease. The name would mean nothing to you. But it has wiped out whole cities in China – though of course, Mao Tse-tung and his lot keep it a dead secret.'

Tottie took a lace-edged handkerchief from the pocket of her uniform to dab the corner of her eye. 'Oh, Lancelot! But you're so young.' She paused. 'To me, at any rate.'

'Tottie, will you have dinner with me tomorrow? Just for old times sake?'

'Of course I will. How could I refuse you anything?'

'I'll pick you up here at seven. Or round the corner? You might prefer that, as more discreet.'

'I think it would be best.'

'I shall try to make it as cheerful an occasion as possible,' he told her gallantly. 'That girl's long skirt, by the way. She meant it as a joke, I suppose?' Tottie smiled and nodded. 'I thought as much. Well, let the youngsters get some innocent fun out of me, while they can.'

Sir Lancelot hurried down the front steps and climbed into his Rolls, which stood neatly across the white letters saying NO PARKING. He accelerated briskly across the courtyard to turn out of the main gate. Unfortunately, a small old car, which seemed to be held together mainly by strips of surgical sticking-plaster, happened at that moment to be turning into it. There was a crash, and the small car seemed to disintegrate into a heap of spare parts.

Sir Lancelot climbed out furiously. 'You idiot! You cretin! Do you realize that you might easily have scratched my coachwork?'

'Didn't you hear my ruddy horn?' replied Terry Summerbee indignantly.

'Don't argue with *me*, boy! I *always* have right of way through that gateway. I know you, don't I?' Sir Lancelot eyed him more keenly. 'You're one of the students. Let me say that if you operate the way you drive, you'll solve the world's population problem in no time.'

'I am not going to be bullied by anyone – sir,' Terry told him stoutly. 'It was your fault, and you know it.'

'How *dare* you. There was enough distance from here to China – '

Sir Lancelot stopped. He shaded his eyes. 'Dear boy, you are right. Quite right. I apologize. Doubly so. My breach of the Highway Code was exceeded only by my breach of good manners.'

Terry gave a surprised smile.

'Where were you going? A maternity case? Some errand of mercy, as the newspapers say?'

'Actually, I was going to pick up a bird – meet a young lady, sir.'

The surgeon invited with a grand sweep of his arm, 'Take my car.'

'Yours, sir?'

'For the evening. I'm sure you will handle it safely, and it will be much easier to drive than your own contraption. Don't thank me, dear boy.' Sir Lancelot patted his shoulder. 'Where were you intending to take this ornithological specimen?'

'I thought a Wimpy Bar, sir.'

The surgeon felt in his pocket for a notebook. He scribbled a few words, and handed the page to Terry. 'Take that to the Crécy Hotel. Ask for the manager. Enjoy yourself tonight at my expense. Life is too short for penny-pinching. I would recommend the grill in preference to the restaurant. Order the chicken *à la kiev*, which I know to be particularly good, but avoid the claret, which has always been unsound. Now I must hop on a bus.'

'Well,' murmured Terry to himself, climbing into the Rolls. 'I suppose one should never look a gift horse in the mouth – or any other transport.'

As he drew up near the hospital steps the clock on the dashboard said precisely six. An open sports car came noisily to a stop beside him. Terry recognized with annoyance the driver as Grimsdyke. The man seemed to be haunting him. He pressed the button to lower the electric window, and said politely, 'Good evening.'

'What are you doing here?' asked Grimsdyke crossly. 'In *that?*'

'Waiting for a friend.'

'Oh? Well, so am I.'

'Good. We can keep each other company until they show up.'

'Now look here, young Summerbee. It is not they. It is she. I happen to be waiting for Stella Gray from X-ray. I have reason to suspect that your eye is on the same target. I advise you to take that four wheeled mausoleum and clear out.'

'Why should I?' Terry demanded. 'She specifically promised this evening to me.'

'Did she indeed? Well, now we can see, can't we?' He opened the door of his sports car invitingly as Stella came hurrying down the steps. 'Here we are, my dear. Punctual to the minute.'

'Evening, Stella,' smiled Terry.

Mouth open, she stared from one to the other. 'Hi, lover man,' she said at last.

'*Which* lover man?' demanded Grimsdyke.

'I... I don't know, lover men. Why, Terry, of course.' She moved towards the Rolls. 'Yes, Terry. He asked me first.'

'Don't be bloody, Stella –' began Grimsdyke angrily.

Her eyes flashed. 'And don't talk to me in that sort of way, lover man, you pig. Let's go, Terry.'

Grimsdyke angrily slammed his car door. She climbed into the Rolls. 'Is this *yours*, lover?' she asked, leaning back as Terry started the engine.

'But of course.' He smiled. 'I always believe in paying for quality. Don't you?'

They started to move away. In the mirror, he noticed with satisfaction Grimsdyke glaring at them behind his steering-wheel.

Still assessing Terry, Stella asked, 'Where are we going, anyway?'

Crécy Hotel suit you?'

'But that's a fabulous place! Since it was rebuilt, everyone goes there – TV tycoons, royals, the lot.'

'I thought you might care for it. I'll have a word with the manager, to be sure of the sort of service that...well, that we expect.'

She ran her fingers lightly across the polished wood of the dashboard. 'We must see more of each other. Much more, lover boy.'

9

Terry drove through the main gates of St Swithin's in a mood of such elation that he smiled contemptuously at the wreck of his own car, which until a few minutes earlier had been dearer to him than any of his other — admittedly limited — personal possessions. But as the Rolls purred through the unsightly streets which the hospital so devotedly served, leaving behind the charmless area of north London for the haunts of largely decorous pleasure in the West End, he began to have second thoughts about the expedition. By the time he reached the Crécy Hotel, the seeds of doubt had grown inside him as quickly as a Japanese water-flower, and blossomed hideously into panic.

If Sir Lancelot had inexplicably decided to press upon him free meals and transport, that was the surgeon's affair. From Terry's knowledge of the man, drawn from the hospital's legends, it might be just another of his famous eccentricities. But he himself had been stupid not to tell Stella the truth at once. It was only the unexpected competition of Grimsdyke which had stimulated the deception as automatically as a reflex. He wondered nervously if he could continue carrying it off. He was unfamiliar with the insides of Mayfair hotels, or of any hotels at all, apart from the long-suffering inns which accommodated the St Swithin's rugger tours. But Stella, he supposed glumly, idled away most of her off-duty time in such places.

As he drove, he chatted in a preoccupied way, the words of confession more than once forming on his lips. Then he decided to go through with it. He had both an admirable determination and a refusal to be daunted by any person or event whatsoever — qualities so necessary for the survival of the medical student. Besides, he realized as he parked the Rolls, it was too late now to admit everything without risking Stella's fury. And anyway, he concluded, it might all turn out to be a bit of a giggle.

'I'll contact the manager,' he said, as they entered the lobby.

'And I must go to the ladies'.'

Sir Lancelot's name at the reception desk quickly brought Luigi from his office. Terry handed him the scribbled note.

'So you are a friend of Sir Lancelot, sir?' Luigi bowed. 'He often sent his distinguished medical colleagues to dine in the old days, before we were rebuilt. I'm delighted that we are still in favour with him, sir. I'm afraid he has not been too comfortable with us so far. For such an old and valued guest, I shall of course arrange for you to have a good table in the restaurant.'

'I think the grill would be preferable.'

'Between you and me, sir, you are quite right.' Luigi seemed impressed. 'Would you care to take your drinks first in the Starlight Bar? The view over London is delightful.'

'I suppose the drinks can go on the dinner bill?' Terry asked quickly.

'If you wish, sir.'

'Oh! And – er, you can put the tips on it, too.'

'That will be done, sir.'

'Do you happen to know a Miss Stella Gray? I expect she often comes here.'

Luigi frowned. 'I can't recall the name at the moment, sir. But of course we have so many distinguished people passing through our doors.'

Leaving the ladies', Stella couldn't resist slipping into a telephone-box. She dialled a number, and said breathlessly, 'Mum – guess where I am? In the new Crécy.'

'What are you doing there?' her mother asked sharply.

'This boy I told you about – he took me.'

'What? The medical student?'

She dropped her voice. 'But Mum, he's loaded. A Rolls, the lot.'

'Now don't you get into trouble –'

51

'Oh, Mum! You know me. Caution to the core.'

'So you won't want any supper when you get in?'

'Not now. Though I must say, these students usually leave you half-starved.'

Tossing her blonde hair over her shoulders, she went to rejoin Terry. Her father though not a millionaire was a hard-working chemical engineer, and like all girls she enjoyed romancing.

In the rooftop bar Terry ordered martinis, a drink he had not sampled before. It delighted him to notice that Stella, despite her struggle to hide it, appeared agreeably impressed with everything. He would have liked to have poured out with the drinks the sensuous feelings which were fermenting inside him, but he felt it prudent to establish himself first as a sophisticated man of the world, someone she could afford to take notice of. Besides, he reflected as a waiter handed him a large menu, he was really dead scared of her.

'Shall we order up here? We'll eat in the grill. The food's better than in the restaurant.'

'That's what everyone says, lover boy.'

'The chicken *à la kiev* is always particularly good,' he murmured, running his eye down the page with a refreshing disregard for the prices. 'Though I fancy we'd best avoid drinking the claret, which is known all over London to be unsound.'

He felt her grow closer to him on the wall-seat they shared. 'You've been around, lover, haven't you?'

'Oh, a little...'

She gave a gasp. 'Over there — isn't that Godfri? You know, the most absolutely "in" photographer in London?'

Terry looked up. A young man with shoulder length hair in a bottle-green velvet suit festooned with coloured beads rose laughing from a table across the room. 'He's coming this way. Would you like to meet him?'

Stella's eyes widened. 'You know him?'

'No, but I'm sure the manager will introduce us,' he suggested, as Luigi himself approached to announce their table was ready.

'Of course I shall present you to Mr Godfri,' the manager agreed. 'He will be pleased to meet a distinguished doctor. He likes meeting distinguished people in all walks of life.'

The photographer stopped, smiled, made a few affable remarks, then looking at Stella asked, 'But you and I – we've met, haven't we? At that exhibition of my work last week.'

Stella fluttered her long eyelashes. 'I never imagined you'd noticed me.'

'Of course I did. I only looked in for a minute, and there you were staring at my picture of the meths drinkers, quite enraptured. I never forget a face, you see.' He laughed. 'I've a photographic memory. Why did you go to the exhibition? Curiosity? Or real interest?'

'But I'm a professional photographer, too.'

Godfri frowned. 'I don't seem to have heard –'

'That is, an X-ray photographer,' Stella said quickly. 'I take pictures of bones, chests, skulls and things. At St Swithin's Hospital.'

'Now that's perfectly fascinating, because I happen to be experimenting with X-ray portraiture myself. Showing the inside of people, not the dreary old outside on view to everyone. It's a bit of a gimmick, of course,' he added disarmingly. 'But you know what the trade's like, love, you have to keep one jump ahead of the competition. The trouble seems to be a load of old health regulations. I can't just buy an X-ray camera and start in my own studio. It seems I'd sterilize half London if I did.'

'If I can be of any help –' Stella began.

'Yes, I think you can –'

'Perhaps the three of us can meet another day?' said Terry quickly. He had grown increasingly uneasy during the conversation, and was trying to console himself that Godfri, being a photographer, was probably as queer as some of his pictures.

'That would be super,' agreed Stella.

'Fine,' said Godfri. 'Next Wednesday. All right?'

'Next Wednesday,' nodded Terry. 'No!' he added suddenly. The others stared at him. 'I'm afraid I can't come here again. I mean, I can't come next Wednesday.'

'I expect we'll run into one another some time.' Godfri smiled and gave a little wave. 'Now must rush to a party. See you.'

'Why can't you come on Wednesday?' demanded Stella.

'I – er... ' He searched miserably for an excuse. It occurred to him for a second Sir Lancelot might be persuaded to repeat the arrangement, but he decided against it. 'The class exam,' he remembered. 'It's on Monday week. I've got to work for it.'

'Oh, what a bore.'

'It is. But in medicine, work comes before play, you know.'

'Let's have some food,' she said petulantly. 'I'm famished.'

Terry's evening went steadily downhill. She ate, he noticed, like one of the starving African children which Godfri photographed so artistically. Her conversation grew stilted. She even forgot to call him 'lover boy'. He cursed himself for making Luigi stop the photographer – and purely through his own big-headedness, he decided. It was only when he was walking with Stella through the lobby and said, 'I'll fetch the Rolls,' that she seemed to cheer up.

'Yes, do get it. I'd quite forgotten we came in a Rolls, lover man.'

As Terry turned towards the door, Grimsdyke came in.

'Are you tailing me, or something?' the student demanded angrily.

'Good evening, Summerbee. Good evening, Stella,' Grimsdyke said stiffly. 'Forgive me for not pausing to chat. But I am already late for my dinner, which I take here every night. And doubtless you will be anxious to return Sir Lancelot Spratt's car before he notices you've pinched it.'

'Sir Lancelot Spratt?' exclaimed Stella. 'What, you mean that noisy fat old man with the beard who came down to have his chest X-rayed?'

'Yes. The number of that particular wagon is imprinted in my memory, since it invariably seemed to bring trouble.'

'I did *not* steal it,' Terry protested furiously. 'Sir Lancelot happened to lend it to me.'

'A likely story! To one of the students?' Grimsdyke gave a contemptuous guffaw. 'Well, I shall leave you to sort it out. Knowing Sir Lancelot, by now its absence is familiar to every policeman in London.'

'What have you let me in for, you stupid nit?' Stella demanded hotly of Terry.

'Honestly, Stella, I've done nothing –'

Grimsdyke gave him a fatherly pat on the shoulder. 'Don't worry, they'll only nick you for driving away without permission, and I don't suppose there's more than three months attached to that.'

He walked briskly away, the sound of argument a beautiful tune in his ears.

Grimsdyke delayed his dinner to call first at the Picardy suite. The sitting-room door was opened by Ted, in his dark glasses.

'And how's the patient?'

'Still in bed, Doctor, like you said. But better in spirits.'

'Good. I noticed you gave it to the papers as influenza.'

'We've got to preserve the image, haven't we?' Ted nodded towards the closed bedroom door. 'I wish you'd talk to him, Doctor. About...well, overdoing things. He gets crazy about young girls, you know.'

'I'd say that was a particularly healthy trait.'

'Oh, I suppose it's all right, as long as they're over the age of consent. Not that it's easy to tell these times. And you can hardly ask to see their birth certificates at the crucial moment, can you? Funny, isn't it,' he mused. 'One day it's criminal, the next day it's fun. But Eric's not as young as he was, you know. We've got to keep his age dark, naturally, because of his image. He looks fine on the screen, when he's made-up and lit properly. His little trouble is imagining he's the same when everything's for real. He'll kill himself one day,' Ted ended gloomily.

'You mean, you want me to give him a fatherly talk – to keep off the birds?'

'Well...not quite so many, and not quite so young. They're active, those little chicks.'

'You have a point,' Grimsdyke agreed. 'Though it's a lovely way to go.' He pulled his moustache thoughtfully. 'All right, I'll see what I can do.'

'Thank you, Doctor.' Ted beamed gratefully.

'By the way, if you'd like to mention my name in those newspaper reports, I've no objection. So long as I can tell the General Medical Council you did it without my permission.'

Eric Cavendish was sitting up in bed in orange pyjamas, wearing his toupee and dark glasses. 'And how are we this evening?' Grimsdyke asked, shutting the bedroom door behind him.

'I guess I'll live.' The actor grinned. 'That girl you sent to massage my back – she was terrific. I never thought I could enjoy myself so much in bed with a woman, doing nothing but lie on my face and let her stick thumbs into my spine.'

Grimsdyke sat on the edge of the bed. 'Talking of women –'

'I know.' The actor threw aside the magazine he was reading. 'Ted wants me to take vows of chastity.'

'No. But he feels if you paced yourself more carefully you'd get more mileage out of the dollies in the end. I've had more than one case in this hotel,' Grimsdyke added morbidly, 'of the girl having to crawl out from underneath when the gent's snuffed it. Very embarrassing.'

'Oh, no! Now you're trying to scare me.'

Grimsdyke shook his head sapiently. 'I'm not. Just think how the blood pressure goes up – the respiration rate, the pulse, the lot. Imagine the arteries taking the strain. Why, it's worse than running for a bus.'

'Okay, okay, Doc. I'll ease up on the dollies for a while. But that's a negative approach, if you'll pardon me. Look at it this way – if your automobile can't make it up and down hills any more, what do you do? Take it to a garage. Not leave off driving. Can't you give me something, Doc? Some pill or something?'

Grimsdyke eyed the bottles and cartons on the bedside table. 'I don't believe there're any you aren't taking already.'

'What I need, Doc, is not stagnation but –' He made a flourish with his arms. 'Rejuvenation!'

Grimsdyke looked doubtful. 'If you got yourself rejuvenated you'd be snatching little girls from their push-chairs.'

'I'll make a new rule. No girl more than ten years younger than I am.'

'No grannie would be safe – I mean, well, it can be done, of course. But it would take time.'

'What's that, compared with the pleasures of a lifetime?'

'And money.'

'Speak to Ted.'

'All right –' Grimsdyke moved up the bed and lowered his voice. 'I do happen to know of somewhere –'

Eric Cavendish swung back the bedclothes. 'Great. When do we go?'

'Patience, patience! I'll have to speak to the medical superintendent first. Luckily, he happens to be a friend of mine.'

'What's the place called?'

'Dr de Hoot's Analeptic Clinic,' Grimsdyke told him. 'A pleasant spot, actually. It's in the middle of Kent. Extensive views, own farm produce, gravel soil, and main drainage.'

10

Four o'clock the following afternoon, which was a Friday, found Sir Lancelot Spratt leaning on the westward parapet of newly-built London Bridge, gazing soulfully downstream across the Pool. The only ships alongside the wharves were small, nondescript domestic-looking vessels with the names of unpronounceable Baltic ports painted on their sterns, washing flapping from the afterdeck and scruffy-looking sailors loafing on the rails. But the lower Thames always stirred Sir Lancelot powerfully. Perhaps the sea was in his blood, he wondered. After all, his younger brother was the captain of a liner, which he commanded in much the same spirit as he had run his own operating theatre.

As he watched, the twin bascules of Tower Bridge rose slowly into the air. They looked more enticing than the arms of any woman. The water below his feet was the oily threshold of seven oceans, and there was nothing – absolutely nothing at all – between himself and far-off seas where the sun burnt its way across an empty sky before setting in an explosion of magenta, where dolphins trundled beside the ship's bows and flying-fish skipped across the ripples thicker than the cabbage-whites in his garden at midsummer, and where there was an island or two with palm-trees and various trouble-free horticultural products, where a man could lie in the sun with his head cradled in the lap of a dusky girl, who smiled and stroked his brow and never even once disagreed with his opinions.

'That's the way to end your days,' Sir Lancelot said out loud. He felt for his handkerchief and coughed. 'Curse this Asian bug! There's lots more of the world I should like to see. Well, I suppose I might have got myself run over by a taxi years ago, or stabbed by some dissatisfied patient with my own scalpel. That's the only way to look at it.'

Giving a last envious glance to the seagulls squawking and wheeling overhead, he stepped firmly towards the north shore of the Thames and the City of London.

He passed through Billingsgate fish market, skirted the Monument and went into a tall block of offices in Eastcheap.

'Spratt for Wormsley,' he told the girl at the desk.

On the eighth floor, Mr Wormsley came to meet him in person.

'Good afternoon, Sir Lancelot. What a great pleasure, if an unexpected one. Splendid day, is it not? Just look through the window, how the sun glints upon the Monument.'

Sir Lancelot grunted. 'Erected by Sir Christopher Wren, in 1677. Two hundred and two feet high, the exact distance from the spot in Pudding Lane where the Great Fire broke out. An inscription on the foot originally describing London's arsonist as His Holiness in Rome was erased by King James the Second, put back by William and Mary, and finally obliterated by William the Fourth. Which just proves that the interpretation of history, like the interpretation of dreams, is a highly treacherous business.'

Mr Wormsley gave a nervous laugh. He was a young, pale, jumpy man in a smart blue suit, shirt with broad stripes, and a hard white collar. 'It's refreshing to meet someone who appreciates the unfolding of events in our world.'

'From which most of your clients are making energetic and complicated preparations to depart,' observed Sir Lancelot. 'As you specialize in the avoidance of estate duty. Shall we go into your office?'

As they sat on each side of a desk in the small, plain room, Sir Lancelot continued, 'Of course, I had your father as my accountant for years. But I expect you know all the tricks.'

Mr Wormsley looked pained. 'Not *tricks*, Sir Lancelot. All is perfectly legal. We do not countenance tax *evasion*.'

'I am past caring what you call it. I am going to die.'

'So am I. So are we all.'

'Yes, but not in six months, I hope,' he said testily.

'Oh! Sir Lancelot, I'm terribly sorry –'

'Look here, Wormsley, I've made a fair pile and I don't feel inclined to leave it all to provide National Health teeth and glasses for lots of people I've never met and probably wouldn't care to. I have never complained about paying taxes – that is like complaining about the twentieth century. The rabble used to burn down the nobs' houses and hang them from the lamp-posts. Now the nobs buy 'em off with pensions and free education and suchlike, a simple arrangement and much more comfortable all round.'

Mr Wormsley looked worried. 'Have you any relatives?'

'Only a brother, who's well off. Made it all from smuggling, I fancy. The wife's dead, of course.'

'You haven't thought of marrying again?'

'Good God, man, between the wedding and the funeral there wouldn't be time for the honeymoon.'

'But it might help from the tax angle.' The accountant tapped a pencil against his teeth. 'In the good old days all sorts of loopholes were open to us. Insurance policies – ' He gave a little laugh. 'You'd be amazed, the number of times I've been called on the heels of your profession, to insure a life which is already departing from its body. "Death-bed jobs", we call them. Some of those experiences were really funny – '

'Quite,' said Sir Lancelot. 'At least I have come to you before I am a corpse emitting horrible odours and accountancy problems. Pray suggest something.'

Mr Wormsley scratched his cheek slowly with the end of the pencil. 'Agricultural land is out, of course. Forests aren't much good. I can only suggest taking up permanent residence abroad. As permanent as your circumstances allow, naturally.'

'Where?'

'The Bahamas? Bermuda? Though they have a water shortage and a racial problem. The Isle of Man is convenient, but inclined to be rheumaticky, and all those motor-cycle races must be rather noisy. Curaçao is remote, but has Dutch drains. Perhaps the Channel Isles. Are you fond of tomatoes?'

Sir Lancelot stroked his beard in silence. 'You are familiar with Aldous Huxley's *Brave New World*, doubtless? The punishment for crimes against the social order was banishment to some small island. I suppose it is now a crime to be rich. Well, it's amusing to think of ageing millionaires making for their tax-havens, like ailing elephants crashing through the jungle to secret graveyards. I'd like to end it all sitting in the sun, but I'm afraid I'm not in that class. Surgery doesn't pay like stockbroking. My first wish is to leave a fairly substantial sum to my hospital, St Swithin's.'

'I suppose we could do that as a gift *inter vivos,*' Mr Wormsley calculated, mentioning another tool of his trade. 'If you could manage to live for seven years.'

'I tell you, I can only manage to live for six months,' Sir Lancelot said crossly.

'Yes, yes… Though perhaps we should execute a deed of gift at once, just in case you manage to get a – er, extension.'

'All right. I had in mind fifty thou. To go to…' His mouth became a firm line. 'To go to my former student, Professor Bingham, for such surgical research as he cares to perform. Get the necessary papers typed, and send them round to my hotel. Now I must be off. I have an important dinner engagement.'

On his way back to the Crécy, Sir Lancelot stopped his taxi in Bond Street to make two purchases before the shops closed. He laid both unopened on the dressing-table while he bathed and changed into a dark suit. Then he unwrapped the first small package, opened a leather box, and turned over a diamond clasp in his long, sensitive fingers.

'Cost a pretty penny,' he muttered. 'But what's the point holding on to hard cash any more?'

The second parcel he opened with more hesitation. He stood for some moments looking doubtfully at the fancy bottle labelled THE EXCITING NEW TOILETRY FOR MEN.

'Got to start some time, I suppose,' he grunted, removing the cap and dabbing the liquid liberally over his beard.

He was waiting in the hotel lobby as Tottie Sinclair came through the doors, her eyes wearing a look of valiantly suppressed pathos. He took her hand in both of his. 'My dear, we must forget my unhappy condition tonight. I insist on that. After all, things might possibly be worse – I could be in pain, or bedridden. As it happens, I intend thoroughly to enjoy the evening. I only hope that you shall, too.'

'Oh, Lancelot! You are so brave.'

'I have no alternative, except to shoot myself. And that hardly seems worth the trouble, does it?'

She sniffed. 'Do they allow dogs in the hotel?'

'Most decidedly not.'

'Strange. I'm allergic to dogs, I'm afraid. There seem to be a big smelly one about somewhere.' She sniffed again. 'An Airedale bitch, I'd have said, on heat.'

'Shall we have drinks at the dinner table?' asked Sir Lancelot, wiping his beard vigorously with his handkerchief. 'The manager has reserved a secluded one in the grill-room.'

They enjoyed a splendid meal. Sir Lancelot ordered chicken *à la kiev* and champagne. They soon forgot the sad reason which had prompted him to make the invitation and her to accept it. Over the brandy he produced the jewel-case from his pocket and handed it across the table.

'A little keepsake,' he explained.

She gasped as she opened it. 'But Lancelot, this is something far, far lovelier than anyone has given me in all my life.'

'Glad you like it.'

'Of course I do! I adore diamonds – but of course, as a nurse I've never been able even remotely to afford them. It must have –' She bit her lip. 'I know I shouldn't say so, but it must have cost you a fortune.'

'What does money mean to me now?'

She dropped her eyes. 'I'm sorry,' she said softly. 'I had quite forgotten.'

'Tottie,' suggested Sir Lancelot, 'how about coming away with me for a week?'

She stared at him blankly.

'Now,' he continued. 'Tomorrow.'

'But…but Lancelot, what would people say?'

He gave a knowing smile. 'What would people know? We were rather experts, as I recall, at the now dead art of amorous discretion.'

'I…I…no, it's impossible.'

'Why?'

'Well…I couldn't get leave.'

'Details, details,' murmured Sir Lancelot.

'It wouldn't be *right*.'

'Must our age group have all the morality while the young have all the fun? That strikes me as a most unfair arrangement.'

'I mean, people in our position. You a consultant surgeon at St Swithin's. Myself in charge of the nurses.' She hesitated. 'Where did you have in mind?' she asked faintly.

'Le Touquet. You know, just across the Channel from Dover. Rather chilly at this time of year, but never crowded before in the *quatorze*. I'm rather fond of the place. It's old-fashioned, but it's instant France – garlic, *escargots*, yards of bread and all.'

'Where...where could we stay discreetly?' she continued hesitantly.

'I know a quiet little hotel where we'd hardly be noticed. Not that I've been there for ages – the staff wouldn't know me now. There's some very adequate restaurants, we can have a flutter in the casino, even go dancing.' He gave a soft laugh. 'Haven't danced for years. If you remember, I was quite handy with the old rumba.'

'No, Lancelot,' she said quietly.

He took her hand on the tablecloth. 'Tottie, I loved you back in those old times – round Coronation year. I love you now.'

She dropped her eyes again, quite girlishly, he thought.

'Let me tell you something – were I to live and not to die, as is so regrettably the case, I should most certainly ask you to marry me. In those happier circumstances, would you have accepted?'

There was a silence. She nodded assent.

'We're getting frightfully gloomy about all this,' announced Sir Lancelot more cheerfully. 'Come on, Tottie. If we find we've made a mistake, Le Touquet has an excellent golf course.'

She smiled. 'I shouldn't bother to bring any clubs.'

11

The dean always believed in a good breakfast. At home he was generally downstairs first, rubbing his hands and smiling as he sat down to his cornflakes, thinking happily of the busy day ahead of him at the bedside and at the committee-table. But a week later – the Friday morning – he had dozed again after the alarm rang, and entered the sunlit dining-room to find his wife, his son George, and his daughter Muriel already at table. The three of them diagnosed with a quick, resigned glance at his pursed lips and lined brow that the delay had put him in a bad temper.

He took his chair, greeting them with a grunt. His wife wisely became engrossed in her *Guardian*. George and Muriel ate silently, staring straight ahead. The dean started munching his cornflakes rapidly, like a rabbit in a meadow. He reached for the first envelope of his morning mail, laid neatly on his carefully-folded *Times* by Miss MacNish.

'What's all this?' he exclaimed irately. 'Has someone gone mad? They regret they are unable to use my television script, though it shows promise and they thank me for submitting it? *I* haven't written any television scripts? Have I?' he demanded perplexedly, eyes flashing behind his large glasses as he looked again at the envelope. The letter shook in his hand. 'It's addressed to you, George. Good God, boy. What do you imagine you're doing? Have you actually been writing stupid nonsense for the idiot box? When every moment of your day must be devoted to your studies, especially with a feeble mentality like yours.' The dean tossed the letter at him angrily, 'Let there be no more of this idiocy.'

George's eyes glowed as he reverently picked up the sheet of paper. 'But they said it showed promise.'

'That is the phrase used, I recall, in school reports when other comment would be dispiriting or libelous. Besides, anyone can write such things.' He gave an airy wave of his hand. 'I could myself, if only I had the time.'

The *au pair* girl appeared with his bacon and eggs under a metal cover.

'Inga, will you please ask Miss MacNish to spare a moment?'

'Very well, Doctor.'

The dean looked round sharply, noticing his son following intently the girl's movements as she left the room. 'I am glad you have not abandoned the study of anatomy,' he said dryly. 'To make up for the time you've wasted in useless scribbling, tonight I shall devote some of my own – which is considerably more valuable – to put you right through the alimentary system.'

'But Dad,' George protested. 'Tonight's the party in Ken Kerrberry's flat. You know, to fix the arrangements for Rag Week.'

The dean hesitated. However much he enjoyed bedevilling the students academically, he was a good St Swithin's man. He liked to see the hospital make a good display at Rag Week, and laughed as heartily as any at the various outrages committed on unfortunate citizens who happened to be passing. 'Very well, very well,' he agreed shortly. 'I'm glad we still hold decent healthy rags in the hospital, with none of this damn nonsense of political protest, which ought to be abolished by law. *You're* not going to the party, I take it?' he added to Muriel.

'Oh, no, Daddy.'

'You'll stay at home to work?'

'Yes, Daddy.'

'Very sensible.'

Muriel was tall, like her mother, and not bad-looking. But at the age when her friends gaily turned themselves into walking aphrodisiacs, she was given to plain hair-styles and dull dresses, striking the medical school as sadly dowdy and old-fashioned. She was a quiet, inhibited girl, any personality growing in the shade of the dean's inclining to be stunted. His glance now betrayed fatherly concern. Recently, she really had been rather peculiar, he thought. Until a day or so ago she had been lively and talkative, more than he had ever known her. Now she mooned about the house like a pools winner who'd forgotten to post his coupon. It was most odd.

The dean's thoughts were interrupted by the appearance of his housekeeper.

'Ah, Miss MacNish. As you know, Sir Lancelot will be with us on Monday for a – er, limited period.'

She gave a deep sigh. 'And how is the poor man?'

'I don't know. I haven't seen him all week. He's busy with solicitors and suchlike. I wanted to say that you may give him my electric blanket.' The dean paused. 'Well, anyway, my old electric blanket.'

'But Doctor,' she said with concern. 'You know that one's faulty – '

'He'll have to take the risk of electrocuting himself,' said the dean briskly. 'After all, in his state it wouldn't really make much odds – I mean, that would be just too bad.'

Muriel rose. 'I shall be late for my pharmacology lecture.'

As George and the housekeeper followed her from the room the dean continued to his wife, 'Miss MacNish will have to go. We really can't afford the expense of both her and Inga.'

'Why not? You put Miss MacNish on your income-tax returns as your secretary.' The dean gave a grunt. 'That's a habit you'll have to grow out of, my dear, once you get your knighthood.'

'I don't like the way George ogles Inga.' The dean changed the subject. 'Sex mad, young people today. Our generation knew the meaning of self-control. And what's the matter with Muriel? I'm wondering if she's developed TB or something. Or perhaps she should see a psychiatrist?'

'Oh, she's in love.'

'What!' the dean was amazed. 'Muriel? It doesn't seem possible.' He glared at a slice of toast. 'Anyway, I didn't think youngsters fell in love these days. They just get at one another, uttering animal cries. Such a pity that flirtation has joined the other dead arts,' he added reflectively. 'You and I, now – we had real fun. Dances and theatres and boxes of chocolates, all that sort of thing.'

Josephine folded her morning paper with a deliberate action. 'While we were courting, yes. Since when have you taken me to the theatre? Or to a dance? Or thought of buying me a box of chocolates?'

'But my dear, chocolates only mean calories, we would look quite ridiculous trying those modern dances, and the theatre is degenerate.' He suddenly seemed abashed. 'I hope I'm a good husband to you? I certainly try to be.'

'Yes, excellent. In many ways.'

'So there's room for improvement? Very well, tell me. I shall try to do better.'

'Do you think me attractive?'

'Of course I do. You dress very well, and go to a most expensive hairdresser.'

'I mean sexually, not decoratively.'

The dean looked uneasy. 'Is this the sort of thing we have to discuss at breakfast?'

'Well, it's more interesting than the medical committee, which is our usual topic of conversation.'

'Yes, I do. Why should you ask?'

'As you keep telling your students, you may be strong on the theory, Lionel darling, but you seem to be skimping the practical.'

'But these days I've always so much on my mind –' He stood up, with a resolved look. 'My dear Josephine, I shall certainly remember to do something about it. Yes, definitely. Tonight. Now I'm already late for an appointment at the Ministry. Tonight, tonight, quite definitely tonight. Without fail. Er...if it does happen to slip my memory, you will remind me, won't you?'

He kissed her lightly on the top of her head and left hurriedly.

As he drove his Jaguar to the Ministry in Whitehall, George and Muriel went by tube to St Swithin's and separated for their different classes. But the dean's daughter did not make for the pharmacology lecture-room. She waited until George was out of sight, turned, hurried out of the hospital, strode quickly down the main road, rounded the corner into a dingy side-street, and made for a small shop with a steamy front-window daubed in whitewash TEAS, EGG AND CHIPS.

The café, was empty. She sat at a stained table and asked the man behind the counter for a cup of tea. She kept it in front of her untasted, tapping her foot agitatedly on the floor. She looked at her large wristwatch. She decided she shouldn't have come. It was stupid, a waste of time. She grew more and more angry, and was on the point of leaving when the door opened and Terry Summerbee came in.

'Hello, love,' he said cheerfully. 'Sorry I'm late.'

He ordered a cup of tea for himself and sat down. Muriel said nothing.

'What's up?'

'You know what's up.'

Terry assumed a look of innocence. 'Should I?'

'That girl.'

'Which girl?'

'In X-ray.'

'Oh, that girl!' He smiled. 'Look, love, I can explain absolutely everything about her—'

'That won't be necessary. I know everything about it already. It's all round the hospital. You must be a dimwit, imagining you can pick up a female at the front door in a Rolls-Royce without anyone noticing. I just couldn't believe it at first. Now I know it's true. You not only drove her off in a Rolls, but you took her to dinner at the Crécy Hotel.' Muriel's lips trembled. 'And you only take me to fish bars.'

'Where did you get all that from?' he asked, looking alarmed.

'Dr Grimsdyke told the whole story on a ward-round.' She produced her handkerchief and started to sniff. 'Everyone laughed their insides out.'

'Look, Muriel, love, this bird Stella isn't even talking to me any more.'

He laid his hand on hers. She snatched it away. 'I don't want you to touch me again, Terry, ever. I don't want you even to look at me, though I suppose you'll have to in the hospital.' She added in a crushed voice, 'And you said you loved me.'

'But I did! I do. That business of Stella was just an aside, an aberration—'

'It's been difficult enough for me already, hasn't it? Going steady with you these few months.'

He paused. 'Perhaps that's the point. All this hole-and-corner business. It's making me nervous. I feel like something out of a spy film, only meeting you in places like this.'

'You know we can't see each other openly in the hospital,' she protested impatiently. 'If my father got to know about it—'

'I can't see what the fuss is about.' He was starting to grow annoyed himself. 'Why should your father object to me? I'm clean. I don't smoke pot. I haven't got a black grandmother. I don't know how to play any noisy instruments. I haven't been arrested even once.'

'You know what father's like. He thinks I should keep my mind on my work till I qualify.'

Terry stirred his cup of tea. 'Look, love,' he said at last. 'That business with the X-ray girl is over and done with. I promise you. I assure you. I'm sorry. Painfully sorry. Can't I ask you to forgive me? And start all over again where we left off? I didn't know my own feelings. I only did it for…well, for a change, I suppose. Like all the boys. Even the ones who are engaged. Even some of the ones who are married.'

'Good. Now I know exactly how you'd behave if we *had* got married.'

'No, I didn't mean that!'

She stood up. 'My brother's been invited to Ken Kerrberry's party tonight. I'm going to ask him to take me along.' Her eyes flashed. 'Yes, I thought that would get you. Ken knows a pretty groovy crowd, doesn't he? People from outside the hospital, who wouldn't cause a lot of complications in the way of making dates. Now I must be off. I have already missed one lecture this morning because of you. And you certainly aren't worth another.'

12

Muriel strode from the café. Terry sat gloomily looking into his tea. His thoughts had become so confused that he was not entirely certain what they were, or if cerebration was proceeding at all. He decided like a good doctor heartlessly to extract the unpleasant truth from the inessentials. He saw first of all that he had been remarkably stupid. He had been in love with Muriel, whom he would much liked to have had as his wife. He had taken a fancy to Stella, whom he would much liked to have had in bed. He supposed glumly that it was a fairly generalized problem. Now he had lost the chance of both.

'Oh, bloody hell,' he muttered. He threw some coins on the counter and slouched into the street. 'Bloody women,' he grumbled.

Hands stuck in his pockets, he made slowly back to the hospital. The first student he met in the courtyard was Ken Kerrberry. Terry steeled himself to tell the full story.

'Pity,' said Ken. 'I was going to ask you along to my party tonight. It's the cricket club dinner, and I'm suddenly short of men.'

'You'll never find me voluntarily occupying the same room as either of those birds again,' said Terry sourly.

'Don't worry,' Ken told him kindly. 'Just in case you should think of picking up the strings again, I'll see Muriel's pushed on to some unprepossessing slob who's unlikely to contaminate her in your absence.'

'I'm not interested. Not a bit. You know, Ken, it struck me this last week what I came to St Swithin's for – to learn medicine, not to chase a lot of birds who don't appreciate it, anyway.'

'I'm delighted to find that at least one of us in the medical school has some principles.'

'It's work, boy, from now on. Work! What was it that Sir William Osler told his own students? "Put your emotions in cold storage." The old fellow was right.'

'Yes, keep your testicles on ice until you qualify. Just think how much better the choice will be then.'

'It's a blessing in disguise,' Terry concluded. 'At least, I can settle down and get some studying done this week-end. I'd almost forgotten the class exam on Monday morning.'

Having so convinced himself, Terry spent the weekend in his room at the students' hostel staring at a pile of open textbooks, and occasionally reading a few lines from one of them. On the Monday morning, in short white jacket with stethoscope sprouting from the pocket, he made up the main staircase towards the dean's wards. His step expressed his usual determination. The dean might once have been his prospective father-in-law, but all that could be forgotten. The only item of importance now was not to let the bloody little man bamboozle him.

When Terry's turn came to enter the side-room, the dean looked up from his baize-topped table with a smile. He was in a good mood that morning. The prospect of examining students always cheered him more than the prospect of a week-end's golf.

'Well, now, you're Mr... '

'Summerbee, sir.'

'Of course, of course. I see you almost every day. I shall be forgetting my own name next. Well, Mr Summerbee, what shall we start off with?' The dean rubbed his hands at the delightful problems he had in store. 'Just step over to the viewing-box in the corner and tell me what you make of that X-ray.'

Terry went across to the illuminated screen. X-ray of a chest, he saw. He inspected it long and thoughtfully.

'Well, Mr Summerbee?'

Terry scratched his chin. Now isn't that typical of a dirty old sod like the dean? he decided. Luckily, he'd heard in the medical school how this nasty little trick was pulled on the students year after year.

'You want my diagnosis, sir?'

'That would be the general idea,' the dean told him coldly.

'Very well, sir. Normal, sir.'

The dean put his fingers together. 'Come, come. Surely you can do better than that?'

Terry gave a slight, confident smile. 'Perhaps you're expecting me to recognize some outlandish condition in the X-ray, sir?'

'You may be getting a little warmer.'

'I'm sorry, sir. I can't oblige. I think it's a normal X-ray, and I'm sticking to my opinion.'

The dean gave a brief sigh. 'Thank you, Mr Summerbee. That will be all.'

'But, sir —!' Terry looked amazed. 'What about the rest of the exam?' An idea struck him. 'Or have I done so well, no more is necessary?'

'You have failed, Summerbee.'

'Failed?'

'If you are unable at this stage of your career to recognize when a radiograph of the chest is grossly *ab*normal, you had better spend the next three months in the X-ray museum.'

'But it *is* normal, sir.'

'Good morning, Mr Summerbee. Please do not waste more of my time.'

'It *is*. I insist you look at it, sir.'

The dean rose angrily. 'Very well. If you wish to start a clinical argument with me, young man, I shall be delighted to put you in your place. Furthermore, you do *not* address members of the consultant staff in that peremptory manner. I must ask you to come to my office at two o'clock on that score alone. Anyone not totally blind, even a seaside snapshot photographer, could tell you that X-ray is most certainly not —'

The dean stopped. He peered. He leant forward.

'How strange.' He stroked his chin. 'Do you know, Mr Summerbee, you happen to be quite correct. Amazing. This X-ray shows a normal chest. Absolutely normal. Just look — heart, lungs, diaphragm perfect. From the bone-structure, a man of latish middle-age. Rather heavy flesh shadow — the patient was somewhat disgustingly overweight. So there we are. Yes, my boy. Splendid. Quite a test, I always think, to make a diagnosis of nothing in an examination, when something difficult and even unusual is expected? And yet… ' He looked round anxiously. 'I distinctly remember, this time I decided *not* to play that little dodge. Where's the X-ray envelope?'

'The patient's name is marked on the film, sir.'

'Yes, yes, of course. I always seem to forget that. Everything is packets and labels these days. Let me see – Oh God!' cried the dean. 'Oh horror! Oh, Sir Lancelot!'

13

Sir Lancelot was finishing his lunch in the hospital refectory when Harry the porter came hurrying across the long room crowded with chattering, eating students.

'Sir Lancelot – the dean wants you in his office. It's urgent.'

'Good God, what's the matter?' The surgeon noticed the man's alarmed expression. 'Has he perforated, or something?'

'I don't know, sir. But he sounded proper worried when he gave me the message.'

'Oh, it's probably something about my moving in with them today.' Sir Lancelot drained his coffee. 'Very well, I'll put him out of his misery.'

He found the dean alone in his room, bouncing agitatedly on the edge of his chair. 'Ah! Lancelot. Thank God. Yes. Well. How are you feeling?'

The surgeon gave a broad grin. 'I might say, my dear Dean, that I have never felt better in my life than at this particular moment.'

'Splendid!' said the dean heartily.

Sir Lancelot noisily whisked a pinch of snuff into his nostrils. 'What's splendid about it?' he asked less cheerfully. 'You told me yourself that's exactly what I had to expect. A euphoric feeling of well-being – your exact words. Then in six months...woomph.'

'Woomph,' repeated the dean weakly, mopping his forehead with his handkerchief.

'Though I suppose now it's down to twenty-five weeks,' Sir Lancelot calculated gloomily. 'I say, Dean, are you all right?'

'Yes, yes, I've just my usual worries –'

'Perhaps my disease is catching?' Sir Lancelot suggested with some enthusiasm. 'You might have it, too.'

'That would be impossible. From you, I mean. You see, you haven't got it.'

'My dear Dean,' said Sir Lancelot gently. 'I appreciate your humanity in trying to leave me with a little hope, but I assure you I am resigned to my fate. There is no need to pull the wool over *my* eyes – even if you could.'

'But you *haven't* got it. It was all a mistake. A clerical error.'

Sir Lancelot frowned. 'Pray explain.'

'The X-rays got muddled up.' The dean miserably indicated two sets of radiographs on his desk. 'I wanted a real stinker for the students in my class exam this morning. So I asked the X-ray department to look out something from the museum. I suggested Asiatic diseases. Rare ones.'

'H'm,' said Sir Lancelot.

'But the girl in X-ray put the films in the wrong envelopes. I thought they were the ones I'd had specially taken of you.' He drummed his fingers on his desk. 'Mistakes will happen,' he added in a faint voice.

'Good God!' roared Sir Lancelot. He sprang to his feet and started pacing the office. His expression, which a moment ago recalled a bear who had swallowed a honeypot, now indicated the creature had ingested the bees as well. 'How in the name of sanity can such malpractice, such muddle, such a bleeding cock-up, occur in a well-organized place like St Swithin's? It's as bad as cutting off the wrong leg.'

'I suppose the girl was lackadaisical, as they all are in these times,' the dean continued uncomfortably. 'She's the rather flighty sort, I understand from my house physician. And of course inexperienced, being one of the young radiography pupils.'

'What's this witless female's name?'

The dean glanced at his desk-jotter. 'A Miss Gray.'

Sir Lancelot grunted. 'And she condemned me to death.'

'She'll have to go, of course. No doubt about that. I'll see the senior radiologist directly.'

'Then what was my blasted cough due to?'

75

The dean looked lost.

'*I* know!' Sir Lancelot slapped his waistcoat pocket. 'I was trying a new brand of snuff.'

'Look on the bright side, Lancelot. You may have been condemned to death, but now you are reprieved. You will live, doubtless to the ripest of old ages. Surely that fills your heart with joy? Why, you have nothing else whatever to worry about in the world.'

Sir Lancelot stopped pacing. He stroked his beard. 'I wouldn't be too certain about that.'

'But I don't follow? You're perfectly healthy. Quite as fit as the entire St Swithin's rugger team.'

'Do you know where I've been this past week?'

'With your solicitors.'

'No. With the matron in Le Touquet.'

Sir Lancelot sat down again.

'Ah, tut,' said the dean.

'Look here,' Sir Lancelot continued earnestly. 'You and I are lifelong friends. There are no secrets between us, or precious few. I can speak frankly. The matron and I lived together in a small hotel as man and wife. We caught the car ferry plane back to Lydd only this morning.'

'Well, you got something out of the mix-up, anyway,' said the dean brightly. 'I mean,' he added quickly, 'I'm sure it was quite excusable under the circumstances.'

'You don't understand –'

'Oh! That reminds me of something,' the dean interrupted. He made a pencilled note on his desk jotter, *Don't forget with Josephine tonight*.

'What are you doing, man, taking down the evidence?'

'No, no, just a little domestic detail.'

'Dean, I can confess to you. I am conducting something of an *affaire de coeur* with Tottie Sinclair. I implore you to keep it dark in a place like this, with everyone always sniffing for the stink of scandal. But Tottie only agreed to come away with me because...well, because I told her I would have married her, had I been going to live.'

'Oh, I don't think I should let *that* worry you,' the dean told him airily. 'The times have long passed when a gentleman felt in honour bound to marry a lady just because he'd…he'd…I mean, people are doing it now all the time all over the place.'

'It is good of you to imbue me with such principles. But there is a little more to it. In Le Touquet last night I did in fact invite her to become my wife, regardless of my perilous state of health. She accepted.'

'Why on earth did you do that?'

'Firstly, my accountants seemed to think marriage advisable. Secondly…' Sir Lancelot took another pinch of snuff. 'She's bloody good value, once she sets her mind to it.'

'Then why *don't* you marry the matron?' the dean suggested. 'After all, she's not a bad-looking lass.'

'My dear fellow, don't be stupid,' Sir Lancelot told him shortly. 'A man of my age marrying a much younger woman really would be dead in six months. That week in Le Touquet was about all I could manage at a stretch. We've seen that sort of situation in practice time and time again. Even the laity know it well enough – businessmen dishing their wives and marrying their secretaries and collecting a coronary on their honeymoons.' He paused. 'Besides, I don't think I like her all that much,' he added reflectively. 'She isn't my cup of tea at all. I was just taken by the way she waggles her glutei.'

'Perhaps you could tell her you didn't mean it?'

'Dean, I am not wholly bereft of integrity. Besides, it might get in the newspapers.'

'I know,' the dean added enthusiastically. 'You could go away to Wales and pretend you'd dropped dead, anyway.'

'What happens when I come back next summer for the Lord's Test Match?'

'Then for the life of me, I really can't see what's to be done.'

'Nothing's to be done. Nothing whatever. I shall marry Tottie, that's all. I trust you will act as best man? A registry office I feel will suffice. Somewhat early in the morning, before the crowds are about.'

There was a knock on the door.

'Come in!'

Terry Summerbee's face appeared. The dean looked at his watch. 'My dear Mr Summerbee, there is now no need to appear before me for insubordination, as I directed. The situation has resolved itself.'

'Might I have a word with you anyway, sir?'

'I'm very busy – '

'I must be on my way.' Sir Lancelot rose. 'My new status as a more permanent member of the human race means a good deal of urgent work. I know you, don't I?' he demanded in the doorway.

'Yes, sir. You lent me your car, sir.'

'Must have been mad,' murmured Sir Lancelot, leaving the room.

'Well, well, Mr Summerbee, what is it?' the dean asked impatiently.

'About those X-rays, sir. It's all my fault.'

'No fault about it. I told you in the ward, you were perfectly right. It *was* a normal chest. I trust you don't want it in writing?'

'I mean it was my fault they got muddled, sir. You see, I was in the dark-room with Miss Gray while she was sorting them.'

The dean frowned. 'Dark-room? What on earth were you doing in the dark-room?'

'I was distracting her, sir. Had it not been for me, she would never have made the mistake, sir.'

'Do you realize what you are saying?'

'I do, sir. I realize that I could have let Miss Gray carry the can, sir. But that wouldn't have been right. I knew that I had to take the blame.'

'And the consequences?' asked the dean sombrely.

'Exactly, sir.'

'Well, Mr Summerbee… ' The dean leant back and put his finger-tips together. 'However much I must admire your honesty and decency, you have been responsible, through interfering with the – er, affairs of the X-ray department, for causing great anguish not only to Sir Lancelot Spratt but to all of us who are his friends.'

'I'm fully aware of that, sir.'

'You have particularly distressed me – ' The dean broke off. 'What exactly were you doing to the girl? No, it doesn't matter, these days nothing is left to the imagination in either literature or life. And, Mr Summerbee, you have distressed even more our new matron.'

'The matron, sir?' Terry was perplexed.

'Yes, on the strength of it all, Sir Lancelot – Nothing, nothing. I'm afraid this is a very serious offence. You will assuredly have to come before the full disciplinary committee of the hospital – not the usual subcommittee, you know, which deals with your student pranks. And the full committee will certainly punish you severely, if only to justify the inconvenience to its members of being summoned to sit on it.'

'They'll throw me out, you mean, sir?'

The dean nodded. 'That might well be the likely outcome.'

'Well…I suppose I'll leave with a clear conscience, at least.'

'I'm sure you'll make your way in some other career, with such shining honesty,' the dean told him kindly. 'Perhaps the Church?' There was a knock on the door. 'Come in.'

'Do I interrupt?' asked Grimsdyke cheerfully.

'What is it, what is it?' snapped the dean.

Grimsdyke closed the door. 'I gather there's been something of an imbroglio about Sir Lancelot's X-rays. I came to say that it was all my fault.'

The dean looked bemusedly from one to the other. 'What?'

Grimsdyke nodded. 'You see, I was in the darkroom with Miss Gray while she was sorting them.'

'How big is this bloody dark-room?' complained the dean.

'Had it not been for my distracting her – delicacy prevents my giving more details in your presence, sir – she most certainly would not have made so uncharacteristic a mistake. I'm aware that I could easily have let poor young Miss Gray take all the blame. But I knew in my heart of hearts it was only right and proper that I should – '

'*He* says *he* was fiddling about with the girl,' shouted the dean, pointing at Terry. 'What are you? A pair of cat's-eyed Casanovas?'

Grimsdyke made a gentle gesture of amused tolerance. 'I'm afraid Summerbee is simply carried away by gallantry. Miss Gray is a most attractive young lady, sir. Summerbee just wanted to save her from the inevitable push. Didn't you, old man?'

'I did *not*,' Terry said irately. 'I was only telling the truth.'

'You were nowhere near the dark-room,' Grimsdyke insisted smoothly. 'You were in the X-ray museum. I saw you go there myself. Let's put it to the dean. Which of us do you believe?'

The dean sat for some time with his head in his hands. At last he announced, 'Dr Grimsdyke – I accept your word rather than Mr Summerbee's. And don't look so smug. I do so solely because long experience of you in the hospital, as a student and member of the junior medical staff, makes the notion of your trying to rape girls in X-ray darkrooms not only plausible but highly likely. As you are one of our doctors, my only course is to demand your instant resignation. Which will also save no end of trouble,' he added thoughtfully. 'If it had been Summerbee, I'd have had the fuss of convening that bloody committee.'

'The letter will be on your desk in the morning,' Grimsdyke promised with dignity.

'Good. Now get out, both of you. And you might tell your fellow-students, Mr Summerbee, to confine their attentions to the nursing staff, who are very wisely always kept fully illuminated.'

In the corridor outside, Terry asked with amazement, 'What did you do that for?'

Grimsdyke laid a fatherly hand on his shoulder. 'My dear fellow, you stand only on the threshold of your career. I have at least got a foot in the door. It is of little consequence to me, leaving this dump. As a matter of fact, because of unexpected engagements elsewhere, I have been rather wondering these last few days how to get out of the place without being sued for breach of contract or something. You've had a narrow squeak – but go on your way rejoicing.'

'I can never thank you enough –'

'Please. You embarrass me. But you won't be offended by a little advice?'

'Of course not –'

'Stay away from the X-ray department.'

Terry grinned and hurried down the corridor towards the students' common room. Grimsdyke watched him disappear, a knowing look on his face. Then he turned and made quickly for the front hall. To his gratification, Stella was hurrying up the stairs from the X-ray department in her white overall, with an armful of films.

'Stella. So glad I caught you.'

'Oh, hello, lover man,' she greeted him without enthusiasm. 'I'm just going to orthopaedics.'

'Mind if I accompany you?'

'Please youself, lover boy.'

They started down the corridor. 'All is well. About those X-rays you muddled up. You have not a little thing to worry about.'

'I don't get you, lover.'

Grimsdyke slapped the chest of his white coat. '*I* took the blame.'

'Oh. Did you?'

'Don't ask me how. But you may ask me why. I did it,' he supplied the answer, 'only to protect you. It resulted, I might add, in my having to leave the hospital myself. But what does that matter? You stand on the threshold of your career, while I at least have a foot in the door. Well?' he ended, inviting admiration. 'What have you got to say to that?'

'Thanks.'

'How about coming out tonight?'

'No, lover. Not tonight. It's my evening for social service.'

'Then tomorrow?' he continued eagerly. 'I'll collect you when you finish work.'

'I won't be here tomorrow, lover man. I'm leaving, anyway.'

Grimsdyke came to a halt.

'I've got a fabulous job,' she told him. 'Assistant to Godfri — you know, that dreamy photographer. Oh, it's *exciting* — he's got all sorts of fantastic plans for my future. Funny, isn't it, it's all because Terry introduced me to him that night at the Crécy.'

'Funny? It's not a bit funny,' said Grimsdyke furiously. 'First you ditch Terry —'

'He'll fix himself a bird,' she said lightly. 'Tell him to borrow another Rolls.'

'And what about me?'

'You can get stuffed,' she said sweetly. 'Lover boy.'

Grimsdyke glared at her. 'Lover bitch.'

She hurried away, leaving him standing in the middle of the corridor. 'I do a whole heap of good for everyone in sight, and what do I get out of it for myself?' he reflected bitterly. 'Damn little.' He started walking slowly towards the main hall. 'Ah well,' he decided, 'that's what medicine's all about, I suppose.'

14

'Good morning, good morning!' said Sir Lancelot jovially. 'Morning, Dean. Good morning, Josephine. My, you *are* looking well! Positively radiant.'

'Why, thank you, Lancelot.'

It was the next day, the Tuesday, and Sir Lancelot came down to breakfast after his first night under the Dean's roof rubbing his hands and beaming at everybody.

'Morning, Muriel. You're looking pretty perky, too. Good party the other night?'

'Super,' she said glowingly. 'Lots of fantastically interesting people. You know, not all those hospital types, who are inclined to be rather drippy.'

'Quite right, you must broaden your horizons,' Sir Lancelot told her approvingly, sitting down and spreading a large starched table-napkin across his knees in a businesslike manner. 'You take my advice, and go to as many parties as possible while you're a student. After you qualify, you won't have the time. Remember, all work and no play makes Jill a very dull girl, and dull girls are as great offences against Nature as wet days in summer.'

'Lancelot –' began the dean.

'And you, George?' Sir Lancelot turned his benign eye on the dean's son. 'You treat yourself to some amusement, I hope? Why, you don't even have to worry about examinations in this house. You know your father hides drafts of all the exam papers behind *The Medical Encyclopaedia* in his study bookshelf?'

'Lancelot –'

'Good morning, Sir Lancelot.' Miss MacNish appeared with a tray. 'I've brought you your bacon and eggs, with some tomatoes and kidneys.'

'Kidneys!' muttered the dean.

'You must eat a good breakfast and wrap up well, you know,' the housekeeper added. 'It's treacherously chilly for this time of the year, and we mustn't catch a cold, must we?'

'My dear Miss MacNish,' Sir Lancelot told her amiably. 'That remark contains three mis-statements of scientific fact – a large breakfast will load me with undesirable calories, the common cold is a virus infection and no amount of outer clothing can act as a prophylactic. But I appreciate the kind thought,' he added, picking up his knife and fork and starting energetically on the kidneys.

'Lancelot – ' the dean tried again.

'How did you sleep, Lancelot?' asked Josephine.

'As a top. Though I'm afraid the mice seem to have been nibbling that electric blanket. It emits some rather alarming sparks.'

'Then you must have the one from Lionel's bed. Our bedroom is so much warmer than yours. Change them over, will you, Miss MacNish? Now I must get going, while there's still room to park. It's my morning for the shops.'

'Come on, George – time for the hospital,' said Muriel.

The dean found himself alone with Sir Lancelot, silently and steadily eating his breakfast.

'Lancelot – '

'Splendid plain cook, Miss MacNish.'

'Lancelot, what are your plans?'

'I am taking Tottie to lunch at the Crécy, and afterwards Bingham is meeting me there on his way to lecture at the RSM. I have a little business to discuss with him. I shall be back for dinner.'

'I meant your plans in a wider sense,' the dean repeated a little testily. 'In connection with St Swithin's, for instance. That suggestion you put forward about invoking the charter, to stay in the wards and still see patients.' He gave a dry laugh. 'You weren't serious, of course.'

'Oh, I don't see any reason whatever to change *that* decision.' Sir Lancelot started buttering a slice of toast.

'Really!' The dean bounced on his chair. Since joyfully breaking the news to Sir Lancelot that he was going to live, he had been steadily growing to doubt if it was such a good idea after all. 'But of course, that will only be until you are married?' he added hopefully.

'Why should it be? Marriage is hardly a full-time occupation.'

'I've just had a brilliant idea. For your wedding present – a world tour. By boat, of course. So much more leisurely. I'm sure I'd have no difficulty at all raising the fare, with a whip-round among the consultant staff.'

'Now, that *is* very civil of you, Dean. Yes, I fancy we'd appreciate that. Much more acceptable than a pair of silver candlesticks.'

'And when,' the dean asked, 'is the ceremony to be?'

'Oh, not for a year or so yet.'

'A year!'

'It isn't a shotgun affair, you know,' Sir Lancelot told him reprovingly. 'Perhaps the summer after this will see us hitched. As it hardly seems worth the trouble of establishing myself in bachelor quarters until then, I shall be staying on here.'

'Lancelot…this cruise. Perhaps you'd care to go with your intended *before* the ceremony?'

'What a disgustingly immoral suggestion.'

'Well, how about going by yourself? After all, it seems a pity to spend an uncomfortable year living here when you could be seeing all sorts of romantic spots.'

'Yes, indeed, Dean. You have a point there. I certainly shouldn't object to finding myself in Australia for next winter's Test matches.'

The dean rose. 'Good. I'll discuss it with the others at St Swithin's. Now I must go about my duties in the wards.'

'Leave *The Times* behind, will you? I rather enjoy doing the crossword.'

Sir Lancelot spent the morning in the sitting-room with his feet up on the sofa, at midday driving his Rolls to the Crécy. But it was not an over-joyous lunch. The sight of his fiancée seemed to dim the spirits which had burnt so brightly at breakfast, fanned as usual by the dean's discomfiture. For most of the meal he ate without speaking, seeming more occupied with himself than with Tottie.

'What are you thinking about, darling?' she asked over her ice-cream with chocolate sauce. 'At least, you've no longer those awful worries about your health.'

'I was thinking about toenails in the bath on Sunday mornings.' She looked alarmed. 'My late wife had the habit of cutting hers there. As I rose later, I would find myself sitting on them. It was most unpleasant.'

'What a peculiar thing to have on your mind.'

'I was also thinking of long hairs all over the dressing-table, lipstick on the china, underwear drying above the washbasin, and foundation cream on the towels. There are many aspects of marriage one never sees until one is quit of it. Though of course, it will be quite different with us,' he added hastily.

'I should hope so!'

'Tottie, you're…you're sure, you're quite sure, you're quite *quite* sure, you're quite, quite *absolutely* sure, that you want to go through with it?'

'Why shouldn't I?' she asked sharply.

'I only meant that you accepted my offer in possibly distracting romantic circumstances. I shouldn't like you to regret anything said in an unguarded moment.'

Her eyes narrowed. 'Are you trying to get out of it?'

'Really, Tottie! What a suggestion. How can you imagine such conduct after I had – well, taken advantage of you. And *that's* not a thing I've done in my life before.'

'I hope you're not implying that I've made a habit of it?'

'No, no, no, my dear…it's just…well, when are we to have the wedding? I thought some time in the summer of next year. Or possibly the Christmas after that.'

'I had in mind next Friday week.'

'What!'

'Perhaps that may be a little soon,' she conceded. 'We need time to make all the arrangements properly. There really is a terrible amount of detail, even for someone so experienced in administration as myself. Let's say a month. Yes, we shall be married in a month,' she told him, with a determination he had forgotten since the incident of the obstetric forceps on Coronation night.

'As you wish,' he said gallantly. 'I take it that at our mature time of life a registry office will be acceptable?'

'Not a bit. I've always wanted a white wedding.'

'What, with orange-blossom and choirboys and cars with white ribbons?' he asked in horror.

'Yes, the lot. Anyway, the ward sisters at St Swithin's expect it.'

'What's it got to do with them?'

'They're to be my bridesmaids. I've already asked a dozen of them. After all, it's perfectly in order – they're unmarried. I think they'll look charming in their long satin dresses.'

Sir Lancelot held a hand over his eyes. 'The whole thing's going to look like fancy dress night in the old folk's home.'

'That wasn't a very kind thing to say.'

'I'm sorry. I'll get married in whatever *mise en scène* and whatever sort of costume you care to suggest. After all, a wedding is primarily for the benefit of the spectators, like any other circus. Yes, Luigi?' he asked as the manager approached.

'A Professor Bingham was asking for you at the desk, sir. As you mentioned you had confidential medical matters to discuss, I had him shown into the private sitting-room attached to my office.'

'That was most thoughtful of you. I'm afraid you must run along now, Tottie dear. Go and tell your bridesmaids I can hardly wait to see the lot of them in their gear.'

The manager accompanied them to the front door. As Tottie disappeared, Sir Lancelot turned to him. 'Just a minute, Luigi. Is your hotel doctor about?'

'Yes, sir. Since resigning from his hospital, he has been spending all of his time – and eating all of his meals – in the hotel. Do you wish to see him?'

'If you please.' Luigi dispatched a page-boy. 'I hope you think Dr Grimsdyke satisfactory? He used to be one of my students.'

'He has perhaps a rather high opinion of himself.'

'He always had. Still, he's resourceful, which I suppose is important in a job like this.' Sir Lancelot chuckled. 'He dealt pretty well with that actor feller – what's his name?'

'Eric Cavendish, sir. He left over a week ago for the country.'

'That's it. When he strained his back trying to roger that little girl up in his room.'

'Girl?' Luigi looked mystified. 'I heard of no girl. Dr Grimsdyke said the gentleman suffered the injury stooping to tie up his shoelace.'

'Then he's got discretion, too, which I suppose is even more important here. Ah, there you are, Grimsdyke. Would you mind leaving us a moment, Luigi? Professional matters, you know. Grimsdyke, I am prepared to overlook that you were the originator of a great deal of mental suffering on my part,' Sir Lancelot continued as the manager withdrew. 'The whole story of the X-rays has now, of course, come to my ears. Well, you caused me even greater mental suffering when you were operating under my directions as a student, I suppose.'

'That's very handsome of you, sir.'

'In return for such magnanimity, I should like you to do me a favour.'

'Anything you care to mention, sir.'

'Grimsdyke – you know that I am to be married to the matron?'

'Everyone knows it in St Swithin's, sir.'

'Doubtless. Well, marriage has a certain sexual element in it.'

'So I understand to be the case, sir.'

'Of course, a bridegroom of twenty doesn't give such things a second thought.'

'You really think so, sir?'

'I mean, they present no problem. But to a gentleman of my age… '

'I see what you mean, sir,' Grimsdyke told him sympathetically. 'The old fires aren't burning so brightly to put enough smoke up the flue?'

'I should prefer to put it another way. If I found myself in the position – perhaps the equally unexpected one – of having to run from London to Brighton, what should I do?'

'Buy a pair of roller-skates, sir.'

'Go into training for the event, of course.'

'I see what you mean! You want some of the old rejuvenation treatment?'

'I dislike the term 'rejuvenation', which is unscientific. But I believe that with advances in endocrinology and suchlike, a great deal can be done to increase the performance, if not the pleasure. I gather – and this is pure hearsay – that certain discreet private clinics exist to provide such treatment?'

'Exactly, sir. You couldn't have asked a better person than myself.'

'Knowing your proclivities, Grimsdyke, I imagined that you would be a mine of information on the subject.'

Grimsdyke looked round and lowered his voice. 'Dr de Hoot's Analeptic Clinic. It's quite convenient for London. I'll write down the address.'

'Thank you, Grimsdyke. It's perfectly sound, I take it?'

'Results guaranteed, sir.'

'This de Hoot is respectably qualified?'

'Of course, sir. Overseas university, though that's hardly a bar to successful practice in England these days, is it?'

Sir Lancelot took the scrap of paper from Grimsdyke's notebook. 'I am very grateful. I shall see you are sent an invitation to the wedding.'

'Thank you, sir. You always did tell us to follow-up our patients, didn't you, sir?'

'Quite. Now I must go and tackle Bingham.'

'And I must go to finish a rather agreeable lunch.'

As Sir Lancelot disappeared in the direction of the manager's office, Luigi himself stepped from behind the reception desk. 'Not quite so quickly, Doctor.'

A pained look came on Grimsdyke's face. 'Really, Luigi, if it's your sinuses again they'll have to wait until I've had my *crêpes Suzette.*'

'You will not be enjoying your *crêpes* today, Doctor.' The manager advanced. 'I have just learned that Mr Eric Cavendish was alone with a young woman in his bedroom.'

'That's right. Not a bad-looking dolly, either.'

'You did not inform me of this.'

'Of course I didn't.' Grimsdyke sounded offended. 'Surely you've heard of professional secrecy?'

'You will have no professional secrets from me.'

'I have certainly no intention of breaking my sacred Hippocratic oath for you or any other well tailored pub-keeper.'

'You are fired.'

'What!' He was aghast. 'You can't fire me. I'm a doctor.'

'It would make no difference were you an archbishop. If I dislike a man's work, I fire him.'

'What, because I wouldn't grass on a bloke having a bit of fun with a bird?'

'I am running a hotel, not a bordello. No guest whatever, not even Mr Cavendish, may have a woman in his bedroom. The waiter should have seen she left the suite after dinner. He will be fired, too. Besides, Dr Grimsdyke, I see that you have caviar for dinner, oysters for lunch, and champagne even for breakfast. If I did not fire you, the hotel would shortly have to close from the expense of supporting you. Please see the cashier and go.'

'But...but where? I've nowhere else.'

'That is your affair.'

'I've a bloody good mind to stay on here as a guest, and put the boot up all of you.'

'I should be delighted to welcome you in such circumstances, Doctor. Though I should regretfully be obliged to ask a deposit for the first week's account.'

Grimsdyke shrugged his shoulders. 'All right. I shall go and stay at a decent hotel. Tell the porter to collect my bags in five minutes.'

'A pleasure, Doctor. And might I ask you please to leave us the bath-towels and coat-hangers?'

With satisfied step Luigi made for his sitting-room, but hearing the noise of conversation discreetly turned away. Sir Lancelot was just coming to the point with Bingham.

'I was always brought up never to discuss money after luncheon.' The surgeon took a large pinch of snuff. 'However, such delicate conventions no longer apply in our materialistic society. Bingham, that fifty thousand pounds which my accountants sent on to you –'

'I have both the deed of gift and the cheque. Everything was accomplished very smoothly.' He pushed his glasses up his nose. 'A very efficient firm, I should say.'

'Quite. Doubtless the money came as a surprise –'

'Not from one who really *knows* you, Sir Lancelot. I am deeply grateful, nevertheless. It was a splendid gesture. But let me put your mind at rest –'

'Yes?' asked Sir Lancelot eagerly.

'I shall certainly arrange for some small ceremony at the hospital, when we shall present you with an inscribed silver tray.'

'I don't want to be presented with a tray. I want to be presented with the blasted money. I want a refund.'

'Out of the question, I'm afraid, Sir Lancelot.'

'What! Don't be stupid, man. You know perfectly well the circumstances of the gift. I thought I was going to croak. Now I've been brought back to life, I must have the wherewithal to support it.'

'Absolutely out of the question.'

'You…you…swindler I I'm not at all certain there isn't a charge for false pretences somewhere.'

Bingham leant back in his armchair. 'Oh, it's perfectly above board. After all, you signed a binding legal document. So there we are. The cash will come in very useful. We can't milk the Blaydon Trust for everything.'

'Very well,' declared Sir Lancelot angrily. 'Have it your own way. Not content with trying to snatch my body, you want to pick my pocket. But let me tell you one thing. I had in fact decided to leave you all in peace, once I'd got through this blasted wedding. But not now. I'm going to haunt your wards, Bingham. I'm going to breathe down your neck in the operating theatre. I'm going to squat in your laboratories. I'm not going to leave St Swithin's until that fifty thousand is all spent – and I'm going to watch the disposal of every single penny of it, with an intensity which would make a tax-collector look like a one-eyed bat.'

15

'The sexual drive in human beings,' declared Dr de Hoot, leaning back in his swivel office chair and putting his pudgy hands on his fat thighs, 'is most interesting. Extremely interesting. What we see, of course, is merely the tip of the sexual iceberg. Underneath we can discern little – just a little – in the murky waters. What, one asks, is this iceberg composed of in the first place? Not homogeneous material like ice. Not by a long way. It is composed partly of complicated chemicals, the circulating hormones of our endocrine glands, which have been analysed and synthesized by modern science. It is composed of the sexual cells themselves, the spermatozoa and spermatogenic tissues, of the ovary and ova in the case of the female. Our iceberg also contains elements of physiology quite unconnected with the reproductive system. Indeed, every single system in the human body, be it the respiratory system, the skeletal system, the nervous system, or the cardiovascular system, contributes in some way – and may I say, sometimes in a *large* way – to the efficient and painless functioning of the sexual being.'

He raised a stubby forefinger. 'So, the whole man, the whole woman, is involved in the sexual performance, the sexual desire. The sex instinct is not something which can be separated, shall we say, from the instinct to feed ourselves. It is all part of the man *in toto*. So what do we look for, as dominating the sex drive? We look for what dominates the person. The psyche! And here again, the study is complicated. The psyche, the soul of man, if you like – is itself the expression of many complexes, phobias, frustrations, obsessions, and so on. But it is the psyche and the psyche alone which must hold our attention constantly in the therapy of sexual weakness. In stimulating the psyche we stimulate the sex-drive, because the psyche controls *le milieu interieur sexuel*, the internal sexual environment of man.'

'You mean, it's all in the mind, Doctor,' suggested Grimsdyke.

'That would be about it,' agreed Dr de Hoot, lighting a cigarette.

De Hoot was a small, round man of faintly olive colour with oval metal-rimmed glasses on the end of his stubby nose, and long black straggly hair which ringed his bald head and merged imperceptibly into an untidy beard. He wore a fresh white smock, buttoned round the neck. He sat in a large room with mullioned windows and a Tudor fireplace, which he used for an office. Nobody knew exactly where he came from – he claimed to be Swiss, though seeming an unlikely figure in Alpine scenery.

'I suppose people tend to dwell on their sex lives quite a bit,' Grimsdyke continued thoughtfully. 'I mean, it's rather more enjoyable to mull over in the bus than your income-tax.'

'Some think of nothing else,' de Hoot told him with assurance. 'Particularly in these self-indulgent times, when people expect to enjoy to the full every pleasurable bodily sensation possible, and perhaps some which simply are not.'

'A sort of "Orgasms for All" attitude? It would add a bit of variety to the placards on a demo.'

'Dear me, yes. You know, so many otherwise perfectly happy young women come along here telling me they're suicidal because they haven't had an orgasm – using the term, my dear Doctor, which their mothers never mentioned and their grandmothers never knew existed, like some item in a recipe. Or perhaps they regard it as some other infuriatingly fallible modern necessity, like the telephone. I sometimes wonder if both were simply clever inventions of the Americans.' He leant back, blowing smoke towards the vaulted ceiling. 'Well, Doctor. When would you like to start?'

'It would be convenient this very evening. I left my previous job rather unexpectedly at lunch-time. A matter of professional principle was involved – I couldn't stay in the place a moment longer.'

'Fine. I have no assistant at the moment. It isn't easy to find a young practitioner who can successfully radiate confidence – which is the secret of our success.'

'It's good of you to offer the job, I must say. After all, we only happened to meet when you were doing research – when we were *both* doing research – in that strip club.'

'You brought Mr Cavendish here, Doctor,' beamed de Hoot. 'More like him, and you will have well justified your appointment.'

'There's just one point – I haven't the faintest idea what I'm to do.'

'You can start by giving the injections.'

'What of?'

De Hoot looked a little hurt. 'Surely you have heard of my famous formula ZX646Q?' He indicated some sealed phials of clear liquid on his desk. 'It is highly secret, naturally. A king's ransom wouldn't buy it, nor torture drag the prescription from my lips. It is an amazingly powerful and quick-acting aphrodisiac, prepared by complex chemical synthesis from a rare plant growing only on the foothills of the Andes. It was known exclusively to the Inzo tribe, now totally extinct – they were slaughtered every one by their enemies, because they were growing so numerous so quickly through their amazing sexual stamina.'

'What's it really?'

'Distilled water.'

'Doesn't do any harm, I suppose?'

'None at all. I sterilize it carefully up in my bathroom.'

'And it works?'

The sex-specialist chuckled. 'Wonders! Come and see.' He rose. 'We shall do a ward-round. You haven't yet set eyes on the working part of the establishment.'

'Nice little place you've got here.'

'I agree.' De Hoot looked through the open leaded windows at dusk falling across the gently-sloping, tree-shrouded neat fields of Kent. 'It was a stately home, left to me because I made the last years of its owner so amazingly happy.'

They went through a green-baize door into a panelled hall with a large table in the centre and some suits of armour round the walls, leading to a thickly-carpeted oak staircase.

'And here is sister.' De Hoot smiled at a girl passing with a glass of hot milk on a silver tray. 'You seem impressed.'

'What a *dolly*. And that uniform…not *quite* see-through, but a distinct improvement on St Swithin's.'

'The atmosphere is important,' explained de Hoot. 'To be surrounded by pretty girls in seductive garments by itself increases the male sexual desire. The psyche, you know, as I said.'

'But where do you get them from? Most nursing schools go in for reliability rather than bodywork.'

'Various theatrical agencies. But a surprising number have played the parts of nurses in films and television productions. They seem appreciative of the generous salary. The stage is, alas, a badly overcrowded profession.'

'But all this actually gets results? I mean, not with simpletons, but with intelligent world-weary old men?'

'My dear Doctor, there are clinics in Switzerland patronized by great writers, great soldiers, great statesmen from all over Europe. You read of them in your newspapers. Serge Voronoff in Monte Carlo years ago treated princes by the score. He gave them extract of monkeys' testicles — ' monkey-gland', you know. God knows what the others inject. Water has at least the advantages of purity and inexpensiveness. In medicine as in everything else, what you want to believe you do. In short, a little of what you fancy does you good, does you good.'

Two laughing long-haired youngsters in identical jeans and sweat-shirts appeared through the front door and chased each other upstairs.

'That is Mr and Mrs Drummond. They are here on their honeymoon. They have benefited a great deal. When they arrived they were so devoted to the idea of unisex, until I examined them I was giving all the female advice to Mr Drummond and all the male to the wife.' They started upstairs. 'I also make a strict rule of no smoking or drinking or rich foods for several years after discharge. That in itself makes for athleticism in the libido department, as you know.'

As they reached the head of the staircase, another pretty girl in white nurse's uniform came running down the corridor, looking anxious. 'Ah, Mr Cavendish is feeling better,' said de Hoot with satisfaction.

The actor greeted Grimsdyke warmly. 'A great place this, Doc. Maybe more cramped than I'm used to — ' He indicated the small plain room. 'But it's doing me the power of good.'

'I'm afraid the nurses will have to attend you in pairs, Mr Cavendish,' de Hoot told him sternly. 'I do not wish to spoil our fun, but we must not outgrow our strength, must we? Remember, we are still convalescent, as it were.'

'Anything you say, Doc. For what you're doing, I'd eat out of your hand.'

'And I'm afraid I must ask you to share your room for your last two nights – we are always under great pressure to find beds, you understand.'

'A dolly?' Eric asked eagerly.

'I regret not. A middle-aged surgeon, one Sir Lancelot Spratt. He should be here any minute. Another patient you have sent our way, Doctor,' he added gratefully to Grimsdyke.

'I know the guy,' nodded Eric Cavendish. 'We'll get on fine.'

'I think I'd prefer to be out of sight when Sir Lancelot arrives,' Grimsdyke put in. 'You see, he – well, he's somewhat conservative in his views of medical treatment. He may take one look at the nurses and walk straight out again.'

'That is something which has never happened in the clinic's history,' de Hoot assured him. 'But if you like, I'll ask sister to show you your private quarters.'

'Splendid idea.'

'Have you any plans for passing the evening, Doctor? We are somewhat isolated here.'

'I shouldn't think it would be difficult to find a little amusement.'

'If you're at a loose end, you might like to join our karate class. The nurses are very keen on it. Some of them could kill a man quite easily, you know, with one chop of the hand.'

16

The following morning Grimsdyke again climbed the red-carpeted oak staircase. As he reached the corridor, two pretty nurses came running past him with expressions of alarm.

'Cavendish has certainly responded to treatment,' he murmured. He looked up, to find the girls pursued by Sir Lancelot in his tweed knickerbockers.

'Grimsdyke,' Sir Lancelot greeted him jovially. 'I think this place is all you cracked it up to be.'

'It seems to be doing you good already, sir.'

'Pray disregard the females. That is only a little game Cavendish invented to kill the time. But I must say, I feel a different man already. It's a remarkable pharmaceutical, that ZX646Q.'

Grimsdyke looked puzzled. 'That *what*, sir?'

'The drug. That de Hoot gives intramuscularly.'

'Oh, you mean the sterile…yes, the sterile injection, sir. Tremendously powerful. It would put a herd of buffalo on heat.'

'And in the family way into the bargain, I should imagine. I do think he should write up his cases for *The Lancet*, or at least publish the chemical formula. It's a crime against humanity, keeping it secret. Exactly as if the nature of penicillin had been suppressed for commercial reasons.'

'You don't perhaps think, sir… I mean, I know it's strong stuff, but there might perhaps be a touch…a teeny-weeny bit…of some element of psychological suggestion?'

Sir Lancelot eyed him sternly. 'Do you imagine that I, with all my clinical experience, would succumb to the suggestive element in any treatment whatever?'

'Of course not, sir.'

'Though about the *specific* effect…the reason which brought me here you understand… I am of course in no position to apply a test.'

'I see what you mean, sir. It's not like breaking a leg, when any nurse will be glad to see if you can walk without crutches.'

'I feel so much younger – exactly as de Hoot prognosticated. And so active. I want to keep running – to chase butterflies.'

'How much have you had, sir?' Grimsdyke asked anxiously.

'I'm on a crash course. Double dose two-hourly, all through the night. Perhaps you should try some ZX646Q yourself, Grimsdyke? Now I am going for some fresh air in the garden.'

Sir Lancelot made jauntily down the corridor. Grimsdyke stood thoughtfully scratching his chin. 'Perhaps there *is* something peculiar about that water, after all.' He raised his eyebrows. 'Might be worth giving myself an injection of it one evening.'

He knocked on the door.

'Morning, Eric. How are you two stallions getting on in the same stable?'

'Fine. He's a great gas, Sir Lancelot. Kept me awake all night laughing, with stories of his operations. You know, Doc, I always thought up there in surgery it was tension and silence, except for the patient's heavy breathing and the clipped commands – "Scalpel, nurse, quickly, or he'll never play the violin again". And maybe the splash of blood and sweat dripping from the doctor's brow.'

'Many a jolly laugh have I enjoyed over Sir Lancelot's generous incisions,' Grimsdyke agreed. 'He's a nineteenth-century surgical character, really. Can't you see him in a frock-coat with threaded needles in the lapels? Advancing over the sawdust with an amputation-knife, as though he was going to fight a duel with the patient, not to save his life? Like a lot of people who find themselves saddled with an image he tries to live up to it, which must be quite a strain for the old boy.' He added reflectively, 'Though I suppose we all do, to some extent. The world would be terribly dull if we just went about being our natural selves.'

'I guess so. I don't care to think what you'd find if you stripped the layers from Dr de Hoot. He can be pretty impressive – and pretty severe. I wanted to leave a day early, and he wouldn't hear of it.'

'It's a strict rule. I fancy he likes the patients to save it all up till the treatment's quite finished.'

'I hadn't got *that* in mind – honestly, Doctor. Though it *is* to do with the little dolly in my room the night I overstrained myself. Hell, my name may be Eric but I'm not a four-letter man. I promised that girl I'd help her on the way to being a model. I asked Ted the best photographer in London, and he said this guy Godfri had everyone crazy about him. So Godfri it was, and she's going to his studio this afternoon. I wanted to be around, because I've seen more photographers in my life than the Eiffel Tower, and I don't want him to start her off the wrong way with the arty stuff. If she's going to model for anything, it'll be canned beans and dog-food. I take an interest in the careers of my little dollies,' he said with fatherly pride.

'Nothing could be easier.' Grimsdyke gave a satisfied smile. 'I've got to collect some books and things I left at St Swithin's. Why don't I go with you to Godfri's place, as a sort of male nurse to keep an eye on you? I'm sure de Hoot couldn't object to that.'

'It's worth a try, maybe. You could easily call Ted to fix a car.'

'Leave it to me,' Grimsdyke told him confidently. 'I'll beard him right away.'

Outside the room, he gave a determined tug to the lapels of his white coat. 'Godfri's studio, eh?' he murmured. 'Well, well! What a nice little surprise for dear Stella.'

Through the open window he could see Sir Lancelot ambling amid the immaculately-clipped yew hedges of the formal garden. The surgeon was feeling frustratingly at a loose end. He was brimming with vitality and good spirits, but there was no means whatever for expressing either, not even a dog to throw sticks to. Hands clasped behind him, softly whistling a snatch of *Pinafore*, he turned the corner of the six-foot high hedge, almost to trip over an oak bench on which sat one of the prettiest young women he could remember seeing in his life.

'Good morning,' Sir Lancelot said genially. 'Mind if I join you?'

Looking up from long dark lashes, the girl raised a hand delicately to stroke her shoulder-length hair. 'Please do,' she invited in a throaty voice.

Sir Lancelot took his seat, hands on knees. 'Lovely morning.'

'Delicious.'

Looking from the corner of his eye, he decided he had never seen a female with such attractive legs. 'I'm glad you favour the mini-skirt.'

'You don't disapprove?'

'On the contrary. They allow plenty of air to circulate round the pelvis. Very healthy.'

'I'm glad. So many elderly people can be stuffy.'

'I'm not elderly,' said Sir Lancelot, looking hurt. 'Possibly in your eyes, my dear, I appear to have landed from the Ark. But I assure you I am very much in possession of my faculties. All of them.'

'I'm sorry,' the girl purred. 'I'm sure you're really *frighteningly* virile.'

'Well, I'm healthy,' Sir Lancelot temporized. 'I could run a mile before breakfast without ill-effect, I fancy.'

'Would you like to chase me?'

He looked puzzled. 'You enjoy being chased?'

'Adore it. Come on!' She leapt up. 'Give me five seconds' start. I promise I won't run too fast.'

They ran up and down the yew alleys. Sir Lancelot thought it tremendous fun – and quite harmless, it reminded him of his boyhood, pursuing the little girls at school out of devilment. She was most athletic, he noticed, avoiding his clutches with an excited squeak whenever she let him catch up with her, until he puffed and started to grow short of breath.

'Got you!' he exclaimed, folding her in a bearlike hug. 'Well, you naughty little girl – what's the reward? A kiss?'

'If you like.'

Then her wig dropped off.

'Good God,' he cried in horror. 'You're not female at all.'

'No dear, I'm a TV producer, but drag's my little weakness. They're giving me injections for it.'

Grimsdyke, searching for de Hoot, turned the corner of the hedge. 'Well, Sir Lancelot! Butterflies?'

'Grimsdyke!' Sir Lancelot released his grip. 'My dear madam...my dear sir...please forgive me understandable mistake...' He grabbed Grimsdyke's arm, leading him away with anxious strides. 'I must leave this place. I must leave at once. I don't know exactly what you are doing to me down here, but you are plunging me into very deep and murky waters where I am not accustomed to swim.'

'He's quite harmless, Sir Lancelot.'

'That's not the point. It is obvious that I must direct my new-found energies into the proper channel. I must marry the matron as soon as possible. I recall that she mentioned next Friday week. I shall agree to that, or this Friday if possible. Perhaps in return she will accept a registry office, instead of turning the ceremony into the biggest musical comedy since *My Fair Lady*. I am leaving. At once. I shall return to London and stay with the dean.'

'I'm afraid de Hoot won't take kindly to your discharging yourself, sir.'

'I don't give a hoot for de Hoot. Between you and me, I suspect he's a bit of a charlatan. He'd have to be, running a place like this. Perhaps I should have known better than asking the advice of a clapped-out sex-maniac like yourself.'

'Really, sir! I was only trying to help.'

'I long ago discovered that asking your advice on any matter whatever was simply inviting disaster.' He wiped his forehead with the red-and-white handkerchief. 'I'm sorry, Grimsdyke. I withdraw that. I am not myself. It wouldn't surprise me if those injections had some nasty side-effect.'

'It would surprise me, sir,' said Grimsdyke feelingly. 'Quite a lot.'

17

Grimsdyke found Godfri's studio disappointing. He had expected something resembling Dr de Hoot's clinic, but found instead a tumbledown converted garage off the King's Road. He went with Eric Cavendish into a small office which still smelt of motor-oil, where a middle-aged woman of clinical appearance in a white overall was sitting over a typewriter.

'Miss Fowler is already in the studio,' she told them. 'As Mr Godfri is expecting you, it will be possible to enter. But please knock and wait,' she directed severely. 'On no account must anyone interrupt Mr Godfri while he is thinking – which may continue for hours on end.'

'Great,' said Eric doubtfully.

'If you don't mind, I'll stay out here,' Grimsdyke said. 'I – er, suffer from photophobia rather badly.' When they were alone, he turned to the receptionist. 'By the way – it's a strange coincidence, but I believe someone I happen to know has come to work in your studios. A Miss Gray.'

'Oh, her.'

'We ran into each other in hospital – I am a doctor, you understand. Perhaps I could have a word with the young lady?'

She jerked her head. 'You'll find her out the back. In the dark-room. And mind you don't open the door if the red light's on.'

Grimsdyke made his way down a narrow ill-painted corridor towards the rear of the garage. He found a door with a red light, which he noticed with satisfaction was unlit. He knocked, and recognized Stella's voice.

He smoothed the lapels of his suit and stepped into a small dank room smelling of mixed chemicals. Stella looked round and gave a gasp.

He held up his hand. 'My dear girl, say nothing. Not a word. Please. I implore you. Let me make my speech first. I have been rehearsing it for hours, as a matter of fact, and any interruptions might spoil my performance.'

'All right,' she said hesitantly.

'Do not turn me out. Gaston Grimsdyke comes today with no designs but the utterly pure one of asking your forgiveness. The last time we met, I was rude. Horribly so. I called you names. A thing one should never do to any female, particularly such a charming and sweet-natured one as —'

'Oh, Gaston.' She started to cry. 'I'm so miserable.'

'There, there!' Grimsdyke briskly gathered her to his chest and started stroking her blonde hair. 'There, there, there, there! And what's the matter, now? You just tell me your troubles, every single little one of them. Take your time.'

'I hate it.'

'What, this place?'

She nodded, blowing her nose.

'It is a bit of a crummy joint, I must say.'

'I've only been here two days, and everyone's so horrible to me.'

'Even the glamorous Godfri?'

'He's *unbelievable*.'

'There, there, *there*.' Grimsdyke stroked her a little more vigorously.

'I thought I was going to have a wonderful life in the studio, meeting all sorts of groovy people. All I do is slave out here, make the tea and sweep the floors.'

'I suppose there's no more glamour in photography than there is in medicine, whatever the idiotic public think.'

'I so wish I were back at St Swithin's.'

'Why don't you just tell Godfri where to stuff his zoom lens and walk out? With the shortage of medical staff these days, St Swithin's would be delighted to see one of their old hands coming back. They were even delighted to see me, and I can't put it stronger than that.'

'They wouldn't want to see *me*,' she said miserably. 'Not the radiographer who mixed up those X-ray envelopes and caused so much trouble.'

'But I took the blame for that. Actually, I was going to come to the subject in my little speech, but you seem to have forestalled me.'

'I know you did. You were wonderful. I didn't appreciate it at the time. God, how stupid I was!'

'Perhaps if you allowed the memory to fade a little, the St. Swithin's powers-that-be in the X-ray line would grow more forgiving.'

'But I can't stand this place another minute.'

'Then take a holiday,' he suggested brightly. 'St Tropez, Nassau, Kabul, you know.'

'But I've got to have a job. I pay Mum four pounds a week for my keep.'

'But your old man? He's a ruddy millionaire.'

'Who said so?'

He hesitated. 'You did, I suppose. Anyway, it got round the hospital.'

She blew her nose again. 'I suppose I did say something like that. It was an act. I didn't feel important enough. Some people pretend they're lords and generals and film producers and things, don't they? You see it in the papers.'

'I've just realized something. You haven't called me "lover man" once.'

'That was all part of it.'

'Stella, I love you.'

'Oh, Gaston!' She started to cry again.

'We can't have you weeping like this,' he said gently. 'Your tears will get into the hypo, or whatever they use. Look, Stella, my love – you want to resume your career as a radiographer. Right?'

She nodded.

'Then I shall see you damn well do. I shall take it up at St. Swithin's. With the dean. With Sir Lancelot. Yes, certainly with Sir Lancelot. I've that old bear by the sensitive bits good and proper at the moment. Unfortunately, I'm now working out in the country – a clinic, psychological cases, very interesting. But I can get up to town again tomorrow, so how about our meeting then?'

'Gaston darling, I'd love to –'

'Sweat it out here meanwhile, and I'll pick you up when you finish work. Six o'clock?'

She nodded vigorously.

'We'll have a quiet dinner – not at the Crécy, the food's uneatable and everyone rude from the manager downwards – to discuss our future plans.'

There was a crash outside, and a scream of agony.

'Good God,' muttered Grimsdyke. 'Sounds like I've got a case.'

In the corridor they found Godfri in his working clothes, which resembled the everyday dress of a Red Indian squaw. He was pulling his hair with both hands while jumping up and down and shouting.

'I'd rather kill myself. I'd rather be eaten alive by wild beasts. I'd rather go and work on a building-site.'

'Where you probably started, anyway,' snapped Iris Fowler, appearing from the studio in only the bottom half of a bikini.

'I cannot photograph you. I will not. You don't even listen to what I say. My God, some of the models may be dim, but you're too stupid even to sit still for a snap on the end of Margate pier.'

'Listen to him!' Iris said angrily. 'I'm Miss Business Furnishing, I'll have you know.'

'I don't care if you're Miss Sewage Works. You're impossible. Besides, your tits are of different sizes.'

'They're not!'

'Look at them, if you don't believe me. It's like trying to get the dome of St Paul's and a goldfish bowl into the same picture.'

'Oo, you rotten old sod – '

She aimed a jab at him, as Eric Cavendish appeared from the studio saying nervously, 'Now, now, Iris – remember, it's just Mr Godfri's artistic temperament.'

'Artistic! Don't make me laugh. He's about as artistic as a foreman down the saltmines.'

'Get out, before I call the fuzz,' commanded Godfri.

'I'm going, don't you worry,' she said haughtily. 'Where's my things?' Eric Cavendish pushed a bundle of clothes at her. 'Ta, ever so,' she added sarcastically, pulling on a leather coat. 'I hope next time you won't hurt your back. Old men like you ought to be tucked up at night with a nice cup of chocolate.'

'I must go and think,' gasped Godfri, as the front door slammed. 'Every nerve is shattered. Completely shattered. Where are my worry beads? Leave me alone, everyone, *please*. I must think, think, think, for hours and hours...'

As he disappeared into the studio, Stella asked, 'And who might *that* be?'

Grimsdyke smiled. 'One of my patients. Mental case. I'll explain tomorrow. Perhaps you'd like me to introduce Eric Cavendish,' he added with a touch of pride.

'*The* Eric Cavendish?' Stella's eyes grew larger. 'But how dreamy.' They shook hands. 'I've seen all your movies. I'm absolutely thrilled out of my skin to meet you.'

'Well, that's nice.' Eric Cavendish squared his shoulders. 'Very nice.'

'In the last one, did you *really* do that chase along the mountain ledge?'

He laughed. 'They got a stunt man for that. I'm too valuable a property to risk losing over a cliff. All those underwater swimming sequences were the real me, though,' he added modestly.

'I thought they were the best part of the picture. Honestly I did.'

'Now isn't that strange. Because it's exactly what I thought, too.'

Stella gave a shy laugh. 'Great minds think alike.'

'That's it. You've summed it up pretty neatly,' he complimented her. 'How old are you?'

'I'm twenty, Mr Cavendish?'

Grimsdyke coughed. 'Er, Stella, I think we must be going –'

'That's a nice age. A very nice age. I think about the best age for a girl to be.'

'Oh...thank you, Mr Cavendish.'

'The name's Eric. And you're –?'

'Stella Gray.'

'Have *you* ever thought of going into the movies, Stella? You've got the looks.'

'Well, we must really be on our way,' Grimsdyke cut in heartily. 'Mr Cavendish is a very busy man, aren't you, Mr Cavendish?'

'I've all the time in the world. Particularly when I'm talking to a pretty girl. Say, how about dinner at my suite in the Crécy Hotel when I'm back in London tomorrow? I could pick you up right here when you finish work. I guess that's about six o'clock –'

'Mr Cavendish!' snapped Grimsdyke. 'It is time to return for your treatment. Or would you like me to explain to the lady exactly what it is?'

'Sure, sure.' Eric Cavendish looked disconcerted. 'See you tomorrow,' he smiled in Stella's direction, as his doctor pushed him through the front door.

Grimsdyke put his head inside again and gave a whistle. 'Don't worry, Stella – he won't bother us. He's a mental case really.'

'Another?'

'Yes. Lot of it about this time of the year, Doctor, as they say. We have to dope him to the eyebrows for his films. See you tomorrow.'

The chauffeur had already started the engine of the Mercedes, but Grimsdyke said from the pavement, 'Eric, I've these things to collect from St Swithin's. It's easier to get a Tube. Meet you back in the clinic.'

'That dolly! Isn't she *fantastic?*'

'Do you really think so? She struck me as rather plain and uninteresting.'

The actor laughed. 'In that case, Doc old man, you must be getting a bit too old for it.'

He drove away. Grimsdyke made for the Underground station, with a look of apprehension which had not disturbed his features since awaiting his turn for Sir Lancelot Spratt in the surgery finals.

18

Shortly before six o'clock that same evening, the dean and Professor Bingham were together in the dean's office at St Swithin's. Bingham was sitting in the dean's chair in his white coat, his feet on the desk, pensively pushing his glasses up and down the bridge of his nose. The dean himself was walking about the room agitatedly.

'It's too much, Bingham. Too much altogether. More than flesh and blood can stand. I shall have to leave to take my summer holidays. Perhaps even to emigrate. I can see no way out whatever.'

'But you were in such high spirits yesterday because he'd gone to the country,' said Bingham in a puzzled voice.

'I know. Suddenly, out of the blue, he said he was off to stay with friends. For at least a fortnight, perhaps three weeks. I was overjoyed. I may even have shown it. Then…this morning…bloody hell, the man's back again.'

'Couldn't you hint that he's not welcome?'

The dean gave a bitter laugh. 'You might hint the same to an elephant with one foot on your chest.'

'He's not the easiest of guests, I'll admit.'

'That's only the half of it. Everyone else in the house seems to dote on him. Miss MacNish, our housekeeper. That dim-witted Scandinavian *au pair*. Even, I regret to say, my own dear wife seems affected. Even my daughter Muriel, such a sensible young person. It's beyond me. Women are completely inexplicable. Possibly it is some form of mass hysteria, like you get in convents and girls' schools and that sort of thing.'

'Must be all rather painful.'

'Not only painful but disgraceful. I've no authority over my own family any longer. God! If I were a man of lower principles, I should ask the bacteriology department for a culture of unpleasant organisms to put in his coffee, and really get rid of him.' He stopped, scratching his chin. 'If I had the post-mortem done here,' he added reflectively, 'I really could get away with it. The professor of pathology has hated his guts for years.'

'But when he's married – '

'When!' exploded the dean. 'That's the question. He told me at breakfast yesterday morning he's put it off till next Christmas or the Christmas after, or the turn of the century, as far as I can make out. And even then, he'll still be storming about the hospital, invoking the charter and completely wrecking our organization. A terrible prospect! And I wouldn't put it past him bringing his bride to come and live in my house, too.'

'But this charter nonsense – surely you can get the Ministry to do something?'

'Impossible. You know what this country's like. Something done by one of our sovereigns several centuries ago without a second thought occupies the whole machinery of Government for years rectifying it. We shall be the laughing stock of every London hospital, you mark my words. The laughing stock of London itself. Oh, God, I hope it doesn't reach the ears of the Blaydon trustees. You know how sticky they are. They were terribly reluctant to give us the money in the first place. It might well be that our wonderful new plans come to naught.' He stuck his hands in his pockets and came to a halt, staring gloomily at Luke Fildes' picture. 'And it's all your bloody fault.'

'Mine?'

'Yes. I had him all softened up to go away on a cruise. I knew the St Swithin's staff would gladly pay the fare. In fact, I fancy I would gladly have paid it out of my own pocket. When he got back from the trip, he might well have left us in peace. As a matter of fact,' he added more brightly, 'he might have picked up that Asian disease in reality.'

'But how do I come into it?'

109

'Because you wouldn't give him back that fifty thousand quid he donated to your unit. If he's going to look over your shoulder and watch you spend it, *that* will be a charming experience.'

'I can take it. The bogyman had no terrors for me even as a student.'

'Look, Bingham – why not just give the cash back?'

'No.'

'But why *not?* We're getting a packet from the Blaydon Trust, as long as they don't consider us as too ridiculous even to hold the patients' fruit money.'

'It's a matter of principle.'

'Principles are all right for you bloody professors who don't rely on private practice. I can't afford them.'

'The fact that Sir Lancelot *isn't* going to perish makes no difference to me. I prefer to imagine he donated the money for the excellent use I shall make of it, not for his own convenience.'

'Bingham, three things – I do wish you'd stop playing about with your spectacles, it's irritated all of us at St Swithin's for years – Bingham, three things can now happen. One, you will give Sir Lancelot his money back, and we shall see the last of him. Two, I shall resign from the hospital and practise for some charitable organization in the middle of Africa. Or three, you will kindly find some other means for getting rid of the bloody man. Come in, come in,' he shouted to a knock at the door. 'What the hell do you want?' he said, as Grimsdyke's head appeared.

'Could I have a word with you a moment, sir?'

'Get out.'

'Honestly, only a moment –'

'Get out!'

'It's about that girl in X-ray who muddled up poor Sir Lancelot's pictures –'

The dean picked up a St Swithin's crested paperweight and threw it at him.

'Must be something on his mind,' murmured Grimsdyke, wandering away down the corridor.

He looked at his watch. The bar in the students' common-room would be open. He decided he could do with a quick pint.

To his surprise, he found the bar, though early in the evening, full of noisy students. As he stood in the doorway, a voice at his elbow said, 'I think I owe you a drink.'

'Ah, young Summerbee. Certainly, if you can fight your way through that loose maul.'

'For that business about Stella,'

'Stella who?'

'You know, the girl in X-ray.'

'Was her name Stella? How quickly one forgets such things. How is she?'

'I wouldn't know. She's gone to another job. I gather she left on her own accord, though – thanks to you.'

'An amusing little incident.'

'I'm sorry we had that row. You know, in our cars. Or rather, your car and Sir Lancelot's car.'

'Forget it. You were just a shade headstrong, shall we say? Though I'd still keep clear of X-ray,' he added sagely, 'just in case she came back.'

'I never want to see her again,' Terry said quickly. 'Because of her, I had a row with my real bird.'

'Really? You are a little old lecher, aren't you?'

'I am.' Terry nodded sadly. 'Though to be realistic, I wouldn't have got far with my proper bird. Her old man didn't approve of me.'

'Good God, nobody's bothered about that caper since *Romeo and Juliet.*'

'It's more complicated than *Romeo and Juliet.*'

'You know what to do, surely? Go round to this father of hers and tell him you're going to take his daughter off and possibly marry her. And if he doesn't like it, you'll both move in and live off him.'

'Do you suppose it would work?' Terry asked doubtfully.

'Without fail. He couldn't even claim tax relief.'

'I'll think about it. What'll you have?'

'Harry pinkers, I think. Largish.'

'Dr Grimsdyke, just the man –' Ken Kerrberry detached himself from the mob. 'We're having a committee meeting. About Rag Week.'

'I'm a little mature for dressing up as a nurse and pelting people with bags of flour.'

'But you must be full of ideas? After all your experience of rags as a student?'

The others gathered round expectantly.

'What sort of ideas? Flock of pigeons in the matron's bedroom? Dean's car on the roof? That sort of thing?'

'A big idea,' Ken told him forcefully. 'Something to get into the newspapers. To put St Swithin's on the map again. We've been rather overshadowed since those sods at High Cross pinched the mace from the House of Commons.'

Grimsdyke shook his head. 'Such stunts are a little difficult. You've got to know the time and place to strike. And with so many real villains about, people tend to put the strong-arm boys round their property. When's the rag?'

'We planned this bit of it for tomorrow evening.'

'I should think of something less –' He stopped. He pulled gently at his moustache, using both hands. 'Have you envisaged a spot of kidnapping?'

'That's an idea! But who? The Commissioner of Police?'

'No, you want to choose some well-known figure in show business. That's guaranteed to hit the headlines. Someone like…shall we say…Eric Cavendish?'

Everyone agreed this would be a splendid idea.

'The more I think of it, the more I like it,' Grimsdyke went on. 'These actors are of course quite used to being kidnapped. They enjoy the publicity, see. It happens in practically every university town they visit.'

'He might have got a bit tired of the process by now,' Ken remarked doubtfully.

'Not a bit. I happen to know he's got an absolutely smashing sense of humour. He'll join in the fun, see the joke. Particularly as he's continually being kidnapped on the screen.'

'And ending the night in bed with a beautiful bird,' said someone in the crowd.

'That won't happen on this occasion,' Grimsdyke remarked crisply.

'There's one little thing,' Ken objected. 'How do we manage to find him?'

'That,' said Grimsdyke, 'is simple. At precisely six o'clock tomorrow evening he will be outside the Chelsea studio of Godfri the photographer.'

'How do you know?' Ken asked in amazement.

'I have my methods. But you can rely on it. I should arrive five minutes early, just to make sure. Ah, my drink, Summerbee. Thank you. Well, gentlemen, the rest is up to you.' He raised his glass. 'Don't forget – the honour of St Swithin's.'

19

To examine the dean's household at six-thirty the following morning – to cut a longitudinal section of it, like some anatomical preparation of the chest or abdomen – is to reveal a surprising amount of activity for so comparatively early an hour on a Thursday in May.

George, the dean's son, was asleep in a small room on the top floor. His eyes were tight shut, his pudgy cheeks puffed gently, his hair, which he was trying to grow, was disarranged over his snub nose and recorded each expiration. Inga the *au pair* girl nudged him in the stomach with her elbow.

'Time to get up,' she whispered.

George opened his eyes and looked round. 'I must have dozed off. It's daylight.'

'I must myself get going. At seven I bring up the tea.'

'Haven't we time for another one?' he asked hopefully.

She pressed her finger playfully on the end of his nose. 'No. You have had enough.'

He sat up, reaching for his pyjamas on the floor. 'Do you suppose anyone in the house knows what's going on?'

She leant one elbow on her pillow. 'Perhaps. Does it matter? It is all quite natural.'

'It might not seem all that natural to my father,' he said doubtfully.

Inga pushed the blonde hair out of her eyes. 'He is too busy to notice things, I think. His mind is always full of sick people.' She sighed. 'Your poor mother.'

'Mum? I'd say she had a pretty good time of it. Not much for her to do about the house.'

'Your father is even too busy to make love to her.'

'Really?' George grinned. 'Funny, but I've never thought of Dad on the job like that. I imagined you sort of grew out of it when you were about thirty.'

'And your sister also is occupied in her mind. She loves. That is easy to see.'

'She's been acting a bit funny these last few days, I must say.'

'As for Miss MacNish – who tells? She is very mysterious.'

'About as mysterious as a slice of her apple pie.'

Inga shook her head sagely. 'There is something strange about her. It is like Ibsen.'

'Inga love, wouldn't you like to stay in England?'

'No.'

'Not working but…well, married?'

'No. The houses are too cold and everything is too dirty.'

'I'm not glamorous enough?' he asked unhappily.

'You are very passionate. Which I did not think when first I look at you.'

'That's something, I suppose.'

'Also you are gentle. And you are kind. And you are quite intelligent, too, you know.'

'Are you sure we haven't got time for another one?'

She kicked back the bedclothes. 'No, I must bring up the tea by seven o'clock to the bearded man like Santa Claus.'

'Do you suppose Sir Lancelot knows about us?'

'I think Sir Lancelot knows about everything.'

On the floor below, George's sister Muriel was up and dressed. She often rose early for a couple of hours' study before breakfast. She sat at her desk surrounded by open textbooks and files of lecture notes, but instead of working she was writing a letter.

Dearest, dearest Albert, she had begun.

How can I bear to think that it will be almost one whole week before I set eyes on your dear sweet face again? Yet I understand. You must be away on business and I should not like to think your boutique would suffer because I selfishly wanted to keep you in my arms. Besides, it will give me a chance to get on with my work. I am doing intestinal obstruction, which is most interesting.

It seems quite ridiculous to think that we have known each other less than a week — six days! How grateful I am that Ken Kerrberry brought us together at that party last Friday night. He must have seen then how suited we were for one another.

Muriel paused, biting the end of her ball-point. She added, *Darling Albert, you have restored my faith in mankind. Love and big kisses, Muriel.*

She put the letter in an envelope, and with a sigh turned back to Bailey and Love's *Practice of Surgery.*

Next door, the dean was sitting bolt upright in bed. 'It's really most amazing. And perhaps a little frightening. I don't know how many times I've had it now — most peculiar how such things slip away from the memory — but certainly it's one of those recurrent ones you suffer now and then in your life. There I am, at the end of this long corridor — always the same, paintings on the walls, glittering chandeliers, long red carpet down the middle. Very impressive. I'm walking slowly in full morning dress towards a dais at the end draped with flags, union jacks, ensigns, stars and stripes, like something at a fair. On it stands Her Majesty, with a sword. I kneel at her feet to receive the accolade, but instead she cuts my head off. Then I wake up.'

His wife in the other twin bed had her eyes shut.

'I had my dream again, dear,' he said loudly.

'What, dear?'

'My dream, dear. About the Queen cutting my head off.'

'Yes, dear.'

'Do you suppose I should see one of the psychiatrists?'

'I expect so, dear.'

The dean tightened his lips. 'I wonder why it is that my dreams are always so much more interesting than other people's?' he asked himself.

At the back of the house Miss MacNish was up in her pink quilted dressing-gown. Like many who live in only one room of other people's homes, she was obliged to keep many of her possessions in a trunk stowed under the bed. She had this out, open, and half its contents strewn over the floor. She burrowed away searching for something which, from her expression, was of desperate importance.

Sir Lancelot in the spare bedroom slept on, as serenely as always.

The dream of royal decapitation made an unsettling start for the dean's day. At breakfast he sat unusually silent. Not that there was much chance for conversation, Sir Lancelot seeming in expansive mood and treating them to a light-hearted monologue about various surgical disasters. The dean's wife Josephine left for an appointment with her hairdresser. Muriel and George both announced their first lecture had been cancelled, and went to work in their rooms. The dean and Sir Lancelot were alone.

'And how do you intend to keep yourself occupied today?' the dean asked sourly.

'My dear fellow, don't put it like that. My life is absolutely thrumming. I've so much energy I could fill every minute twice over with activity of some sort or another. I fancy I shall pass the morning writing letters. And this afternoon –' A glint came into his eye. 'I shall go to St Swithin's to mooch round Bingham's wards.'

'You're not *really* exercising your rights under the charter? Won't you have second thoughts, Lancelot? And some consideration for the rest of us, trying to perform our difficult tasks in the hospital, which is already at sixes and sevens through the rebuilding? I implore you to forget the harebrained idea. Can't I appeal to your better nature?' he ended hopefully.

'I have no nature better than my everyday one, enjoyed by the world in general. I don't see why I shouldn't care for a patient or two of Bingham's. It's not that I'm asking to be paid for it. On the contrary, I am giving fifty thousand quid for the privilege.' He poured himself another cup of coffee. 'No, Dean, I will not renounce my rights. Indeed, I should be very surprised if by tonight I haven't the knife in my hand again.'

The dean groaned. 'Perhaps marriage will have some effect on your strong views?'

'None whatsoever.'

'When's the ceremony, anyway? Not for some months, you said.'

'Did I? You must have misunderstood me. It's a week tomorrow.'

'So soon?'

'No time to waste, I feel. I telephoned Tottie last night, and she is going ahead with the arrangements. She's extremely efficient at the admin stuff, naturally. I have fortunately persuaded her to hold the party in a registry office, though quite a gaggle will be coming along to see the fun.'

'If you would still like to take up my offer of a free world cruise for your honeymoon, I'm sure it could be arranged even at this short notice.'

'I'll think about it. Though I don't want to be too long away from St Swithin's. A fellow like Bingham, with absolutely no sense of the value of money, could spend the cash in a jiffy behind my back.'

The dean was looking puzzled. 'I'm sure I didn't get you wrong, Lancelot. You were so definite the wedding wouldn't be for months, or even years. That trip to your friends in the country seems to have changed you considerably.'

'I didn't go to friends. I can tell *you*, Dean – after all, you're to be my best man. I went to a place for sexual rejuvenation.'

'Good God.'

'Dr de Hoot's Analeptic Clinic. In Kent. And damn good it is, too.'

'Good God.'

'There's a preparation they use – secret formula, of course – which makes you feel a new man. A much younger new man.'

'Good God.'

'You seem shocked.'

'I think I am entitled to be. For you, a professional man, a man of status –'

'But I told you, marriage to a younger woman for a man of my age is a damn sight riskier than taking up motor-racing at Brands Hatch. I need all the help I can get. Those injections could prove absolutely life-saving. Besides, my dear Dean, all my career I've tried to leave my patients entirely satisfied, and I see no reason to abandon my principles now.'

The dean rose. 'That's your affair, I suppose. Now I must be off to the hospital. I've a ward-round at ten.'

'Leave *The Times*, will you? I like to amuse myself with the crossword.'

The dean made for the door. He paused. '*What* did you say the name of that place was?'

'Dr de Hoot's Analeptic Clinic.'

'H'm,' said the dean thoughtfully, leaving the room.

Sir Lancelot started reading the dean's paper. He looked up as he heard a gentle click. Muriel had softly slipped into the dining-room and was standing against the closed door, breathing heavily.

'Sir Lancelot, could I have a word with you?'

'Certainly, my dear. Come to something tricky in your surgery?'

'It's not about work. It's about men.'

'Much more interesting.'

'You see, I am in love.'

'Don't look so worried about it. It's an endemic condition at your age.'

'At least, I think I am. I thought I was once before, then I thought I wasn't. Now I'm worried that I'll think that I was only thinking I was once again. Though I don't really think so.'

'Quite.' Sir Lancelot stroked his beard.

'What do you think?'

'Someone in the hospital?' She shook her head vigorously. 'Socially acceptable?'

'Oh, yes. He runs an antique boutique.'

'Wants to marry you?'

She lowered her eyes. 'I don't know. But the other night he took me to a discotheque and then asked me back to his place – he lives over the boutique – for a…well, Sir Lancelot, I'm not frigid or anything like that, and I know a lot of girls do, I mean, quite nice girls, but I don't know…I suppose I've had rather a lot of brainwashing on the subject from father,' she ended a little pathetically.

'My dear, don't apologize for your morals. Anyway, the pleasures of self-discipline are sadly underestimated. Nothing is quite so delightful as a feeling of smugness.'

'But if I don't let him, he'll think I don't love him.'

'There are surely other ways of expressing your appreciation of his attentions?'

'What other ways?'

'Taking an interest in his work, let us say. Men always find that flattering, whether they're safebreakers or surgeons. He's an antique seller? Well, think of some means you can help him with this somewhat esoteric occupation.'

Muriel looked brighter. 'Yes, I'm sure I can find something. I'm so glad I thought of asking you. I could have gone to father with the problem, of course, but he seems to think that I shouldn't have any sort of sex life before I have some letters after my name. You won't tell him I've spoken to you, will you?' she added anxiously. 'I've already had to fib this morning about my lecture being cancelled.'

'I have the discretion of a particularly taciturn oyster.'

Once alone, he produced his pencil and started on the crossword. He had briskly changed an able cop into a placebo when he became uneasily aware of some other living creature in the room. He looked up expecting to find Miss MacNish's cat, but instead encountered George staring with his large glasses through the doorway.

'Either come in or go out, but kindly shut that ruddy door before I die of frostbite.'

George jumped inside, shut the door with a quick motion, and stood against it in the attitude of a timid spy facing the firing-squad. Sir Lancelot looked at him bleakly. He was less well disposed to clamant young men than young women.

'I presume you told a lie this morning, about your lecture being cancelled?'

George looked alarmed. 'How did you know that, Sir Lancelot?'

'Let us not concern ourselves. I take it you want my advice about something? Money, women, or drugs?'

'Oh, neither, Sir Lancelot…though perhaps it's a woman, in a way. The fact is, I want to give up medicine.'

'I fail to see the connection.'

'I want to get married. Please don't ask to whom –'

'The *au pair* girl. Go on.'

George licked his lips. 'So I want to make some money *now*. I want to be independent. Of father. I think he'd like me to get my Fellowship in surgery before I even took a bird to the movies.'

'And how do you propose to acquire this independence? Hawking encyclopedias at the door?'

'Script-writing. For the box. I've had a couple of sketches on already. Under another name, of course, so dad wouldn't know. I'm sure I've got a future in it. And I'm not cut out for medicine at all. Dad only made me go in for it because he couldn't think what else to do with me. I'm not like Muriel. She's a real Elizabeth Garrett Anderson. But of course dad won't hear of me leaving St Swithin's. So what am I going to do?' he ended imploringly.

'It is a matter of supreme indifference to me what you do –' Sir Lancelot paused. He gave a smile. The chance of a little harmless fun at the dean's expense occurred to him. 'The answer is perfectly simple. If you can't voluntarily get out of St Swithin's you can always have yourself chucked out of the place.'

'But how could I possibly manage that?'

'Good grief, man, are you modern students lilylivered, or simply lacking in imagination? When I was a lad, we had to bend all our efforts simply to avoid that particular fate every Saturday night.'

George scratched his head. 'All right,' he said firmly. 'I'll do my best. That is, my worst.'

'And good luck to you.'

George scuttled away guiltily as the housekeeper appeared.

'What is it, Miss MacNish?'

'I've made another Dundee cake, Sir Lancelot. I wondered if you'd care for a slice or two with your morning coffee?'

'Calories, calories,' he sighed. 'But it would be most acceptable.'

'And what would you like for your dinner tonight? It's a long time past Burns' Night, but I know you're fond of haggis.'

'It always makes the dean sick.'

'Och, I'll boil him an egg. It won't do him any harm. Would you believe it, Sir Lancelot, he locked away the best brandy? I've switched the bottles back again. To think of you having to drink the cheap stuff!' She started clearing up the dishes. 'I *am* glad you decided to stay with the dean. They're a nice enough family, but it's not the same as looking after a real gentleman. I look back on those days as the happiest in my life, I really do. Oh, there's someone waiting to see you. A Dr Grimsdyke.'

Sir Lancelot's eyebrows shot up. 'I wonder what he's after? You'd better show him in.'

Grimsdyke sat at the breakfast-table and accepted a cup of lukewarm coffee. He came to the point at once. 'It's about Miss Gray, sir. The girl who muddled up your X-rays. She wants her old job back at St Swithin's. I wondered if you'd put in a good word for her?'

'Me? The victim?'

'It wasn't really her fault, sir, but mine. And I particularly think she deserves a career. I intend myself to do some proper medicine again in hospital, which isn't very well paid.'

'I fail to see the connection, but both projects seem praiseworthy enough.' He thought for some moments. 'I'll see if the senior radiologist is in a forgiving frame of mind. It's the least I can do for you, I suppose, after that splendid treatment you arranged for me in the clinic.'

Grimsdyke looked concerned. 'I hoped you were doing this more as a personal favour than a return for professional services.'

'Why should you say that? Those injections were absolutely terrific. It was quite embarrassing this morning when the little Swedish girl brought in my early cup of tea.'

'Sir...you suggested the formula should be published in the medical Press. Would you like me to disclose it to you?'

'I'd be very interested. Though don't forget I'm a surgeon, not a biochemist. I can't understand a lot of complicated chemical symbols.'

'I think you'll understand this one, sir. It's H_2O.'

'What!'

Grimsdyke tapped his forehead. 'The effect is felt up here, sir. Very powerfully.'

'To think! De Hoot was charging twenty pounds a jab for them.'

'That's all part of the treatment, sir.'

Sir Lancelot slumped in his chair. 'You're quite right – the effect has left me. Gone. Pht. Just like that.'

'I thought you should know the truth, sir. As a matter of fact, I never thought the hocus-pocus would work on you.'

'I appreciate your frankness.' Sir Lancelot suddenly sounded weary. 'It was an honourable gesture on your part.'

'Thank you, sir.'

There was a pause. 'Very well. No more can be done or said about it. I am going to St Swithin's this afternoon. I shall put in a word for your radiographer. Now leave me. I want to think.'

Grimsdyke rose awkwardly. 'Good-bye, sir.'

'Good-bye, Grimsdyke,' said Sir Lancelot in a voice of doom.

He sat for some minutes staring blankly at the remains of his breakfast. 'I feel so old,' he muttered. 'So old. And I'm to be married. On Friday week. Oh God!'

20

Just before six o'clock that evening, Eric Cavendish was being driven in the Mercedes down a Chelsea street leading towards Godfri's studios in the converted garage. Like all London side-streets, the kerbs were lined by an unbroken row of parked cars, which the chauffeur searched hopefully for a gap.

'Double-park here a minute,' the actor instructed him. 'If the fuzz show up, just say it's Eric Cavendish.'

He climbed out, flicking a speck from his stylish new suit. He had prepared himself with particular care that evening. For his last day at Dr de Hoot's clinic he had asked for double doses of injections, and every time the needle went in he thought of twenty-year-old Stella.

He squeezed himself between two cars, walked jauntily a few yards along the pavement, then turned into a short road between two high buildings which led to the studio. He noticed two men in white coats standing in the middle of this passageway, between them on the ground a white-painted metal drum the size of a pressurized beer-cask. Their attitude vaguely struck him as strange. They had their heads cocked and seemed to be listening to it.

'Good evening,' he called genially.

'Oh, sir!' cried one of the white-coated figures in alarm. 'Do you know where you are?'

'In Chelsea, London, I guess.'

'How terrible!' exclaimed the other. 'You just stepped right into it.'

Eric Cavendish came to a halt, frowning. 'Into what?'

'Didn't you see?' said the first urgently. 'The notice.'

Eric Cavendish's eyes followed his agitated finger in the direction of a large white card set against the opposite wall.

METROPOLITAN POLICE
DANGER!
RADIOACTIVITY
KEEP OUT!

'What's this?' he asked in puzzlement. 'Has the bomb dropped, or something?'

'There's been an accident,' the second man told him. 'Most unfortunate. Van taking radioisotopes to the hospital – run into by a taxi – right there on the corner – container split open – stuff all over the shop.'

'It's 131-iodine.'

'Emits beta and gamma radiation.'

'Half-life of eight days.'

'Settles in the thyroid gland.'

'Is there any danger?' Eric Cavendish falteringly asked the smaller of the two.

'Danger!' Terry Summerbee gave a short laugh. 'He asks if there's any *danger*, Doctor!'

'I shouldn't like to be in that poor soul's shoes, eh, Doctor?' agreed Ken Kerrberry more grimly.

'That's the Geiger counter.' Terry indicated the metal cask. 'Just you listen.'

Eric Cavendish held his breath. He heard a ticking as loud as a cheap alarm-clock.

'Now, wait a minute...' The actor looked anxiously from one to the other. They were clearly doctors – they had stethoscopes sticking from the pockets of their white coats. They were young, but he supposed those clever researchers in radioactivity generally were. They spoke in an extremely learned fashion. 'But what about you two?' he demanded. 'Shouldn't you be dressed up like a couple of astronauts?'

'*We*'re all right,' Terry told him. 'We've taken the antidote.'

'That's 14-carbon,' Ken said briefly. 'Half-life, five thousand six hundred years.'

'But…but what are the effects?'

'Sterility, derangement of the germ-plasm, and impotence.'

Oh, no!

'That's for a start,' Terry added. 'The long-term ones I should hesitate to mention.'

'What am I to do?' Eric Cavendish cried hopelessly.

'Thank God, we can save you.'

'You must be decontaminated instantly.'

'I'll do anything, Doctor…but right now,' he remembered, 'I've got a date.'

'Instantly,' Ken repeated. 'Or I certainly can't be answerable for the consequences.'

'Nor I,' Terry agreed. 'To you or to unborn generations.'

'Here comes the ambulance now.'

'Thank heavens, Doctor! The patient's in luck.'

'Not a moment to lose.'

'Already it may be too late.'

Eric Cavendish looked anxiously at the door of the studio, then at an ambulance backing into the cul-de-sac. 'I've got a car and a chauffeur.'

'A chauffeur!' said Ken. 'Poor man. Tell him to drive away instantly. He may still be all right. In we get. Doctor, don't forget the Geiger counter.'

'Where are you taking me?' asked Eric Cavendish in anguish.

'St Swithin's Hospital. We specialize in cases like yours.'

The actor shouted some instructions to his chauffeur. The ambulance doors clanged. It drove at speed towards St Swithin's, with all the policemen holding up the traffic.

Stella was already waiting outside the studio when a few minutes later Grimsdyke turned the corner. 'Sorry I'm late, love,' he said cheerfully. 'I hope you were expecting me?'

'Of course I was, Gaston.'

'And no one else?'

She hesitated just a second. 'No, no one else at all.'

'Not this Eric Cavendish bloke?' She pressed against his chest. 'I don't suppose he's even thinking of you now –'

She broke away. 'That notice – against the wall!' He inspected it and laughed. 'Oh, that? Probably some student joke.'

Eric Cavendish was certainly not thinking of Stella, nor of anything except himself. He lay on a stretcher in the ambulance while the two doctors discussed his case between themselves. Though he was lost with the medical terminology, everything they said seemed progressively frightening.

'Am I going to live?' he cried.

'That remains to be seen.'

'Oh, God.'

'Science will do its best for you, of course.'

'But why wasn't there some warning – something on TV or the radio?'

'You mean you didn't hear it?'

'Oh, God.'

The ambulance stopped and reversed.

'Here we are,' said Terry. 'What's your name, by the way?'

'Eric Cavendish.'

'E Cavendish. Right. You'll be quiet, won't you? The hospital is full of radioactive cases, all seriously ill and a good many of them dying. This way.'

Eric Cavendish stepped out. He was outside a forbidding-looking hospital building. His escorts hurried him through a small side-door reserved, they explained, for contaminated cases. It led to a plain, long empty corridor with two or three wheel-chairs and trolleys stored in it. Terry opened another door. 'This is the decontamination room.' It was a cubicle with only a table, a hard chair and a clinical couch. 'Now take your clothes off.'

'Clothes? All of them?'

'Of course. They go to the fabric decontamination centre. We will be back to decontaminate you later.'

'But supposing someone else walked in? A nurse, or someone.'

'Don't worry, we'll lock the door.'

'Thank you, Doctor.' It occurred to Eric Cavendish that in the panic he had not expressed gratitude to his saviours. 'I'm very grateful to you both, for your life-saving action.'

'All part of the day's work,' Terry told him cheerfully. 'By the way, I think we'd better take that corset affair, too.'

They left him alone. He heard the key turn in the lock. He sat down gingerly on the hard chair and put his elbows on the table. It occurred to him that he had omitted to ask exactly how long they would be. He wished he had a cigarette. He looked round hopefully for something to pass the time. There was a leaflet on the floor in the corner, which he picked up and found to be headed POSTNATAL EXERCISES FOR MOTHERS. It seemed a strange thing to find in such a ghoulish place. He sat down again and shivered.

21

At that same moment, Sir Lancelot Spratt was advancing purposefully across the open space behind the main hospital building towards the new surgical block, a gloomy but stern look on his face. This intensified as he noticed his bride-to-be in her uniform, walking through the automatic doors just ahead of him. He stroked his beard and grunted. Then rearranging his features into one of unctuous charm, he lengthened his stride to catch her.

'Hello, Tottie, my dear. What a pleasant surprise! I'm just up to Professor Bingham's ward to refresh eye and hand with a few of his cases.'

'Hello, Lancelot. I'm on my way up there, too. Sister's off sick, and the new staff nurse seems to be making rather heavy weather of it.'

They reached the lift. Sir Lancelot gave a deep sigh. 'It seems such a waste.'

'I don't think I follow.'

He pressed the button for the top floor. 'You, Tottie, a highly trained and most experienced member of the nursing profession, from tomorrow week will be lost to humanity.'

'But Lancelot, you know how much I shall prefer looking after you.'

'Doubtless, doubtless. But it does seem a tragedy, that's all.'

'What do you want me to do? Carry on with my job? Lady Spratt, a working wife?'

'No, no. I'd never suggest a thing like that.'

'Perhaps you'd kindly tell me what you *are* suggesting?'

'You might possibly – bearing in mind the undeniable success of your career and the uncountable benefits it has bestowed – think twice before abandoning it for such a mundane institution as marriage?'

'No.'

'I mean, the world contains few matrons but many wives.'

'What the hell are you getting at? You're quite beyond me, Lancelot. First you want the wedding next year, then you agree to a couple of months, then you ring me up to say you can hardly wait and we've got to get married next week. Can't you make up your mind?'

'It is a big step in one's life, deserving a great deal of thought.'

They reached the top floor.

'You're not trying to get out of it again, are you?'

'I? Perish the thought.'

'I should damn well hope so.' She moved away with a determined step. 'Because you're not going to.'

'Sir Lancelot – ' Bingham in his white coat was standing outside the lift. 'I understand from my house surgeon that you intend to operate this evening on an inguinal hernia from my wards.'

'Quite so. It is a comparatively simple operation, just what I need for flexing my surgical muscles again. The houseman assures me there is a case in, even though the patient happens to have been admitted for something quite different. I suppose you do your hernias these days as out-patients? It will be an unexpected bonus for the man's stay in hospital.'

'I'm afraid you are mistaken. The theatre is not available for you.'

'On the contrary, Bingham, I have told the theatre sister to prepare for the case in ten minutes. I shall examine the patient pre-operatively in the anaesthetic room.'

'I have countermanded your orders.'

'How dare you! You know perfectly well my rights under the terms of the charter.'

'The charter doesn't give you any right to upset everybody in the hospital. Not only the staff and the nurses, who can take it. But the patients, who can't. On their behalf, I ask you to get out of my wards at once.'

'You do, do you? Well, if you're acting only for high-minded humanitarian reasons, I shall accede. At a price.'

'What price?'

'My fifty thousand quid.'

'I refuse to submit to blackmail.'

'Blackmail! When every single penny piece of it's my own?'

'You will leave my wards, and without a single condition –'

They were interrupted by the lift door opening. It emitted the dean, Harry the porter, and a fat man in a blue uniform and chauffeur's cap.

'Bingham! Thank God. Something terrible has happened –'

'If you'll forgive me,' said Sir Lancelot loftily, moving away, 'I shall be about my duties.'

'Yes, please, Lancelot, leave us,' said the dean distractedly. 'It's the students, Bingham.'

'What are you getting excited about? It's Rag Week,' Bingham said impatiently.

'In the usual way, I wouldn't be excited, no. A joke's a joke, and I'm the first to laugh. But this time…I'll explain. Do you know a film actor called Eric Chatterley?'

'Eric Cavendish,' the chauffeur corrected him.

'Exactly. He was driven away from somewhere in Chelsea in an ambulance. It was very strange. He hadn't been ill or had an accident or anything.'

'I thought I'd better follow up, sir,' said the chauffeur. 'The poor gentleman might want his relatives informed.'

'And there's not so much as a smell of him in the hospital, sir,' added Harry.

'You've checked in casualty?' asked Bingham.

'Twice, sir.'

'You see, it's the students,' said the dean. 'Kidnapping. Dear me, dear me! If anything happened to the fellow, there'd be the devil to pay. He must be valued in millions of dollars.'

'Summerbee and Kerrberry.' Bingham stopped the two students trying to sidle unseen into the lift. 'Do you know anything about this?'

'Oh, no, sir.'

'But you're on the Rag Week committee, aren't you?'

'Yes, sir. But we decided this year just to put a live alligator in the Serpentine.'

'Perhaps we'd better search the hospital, Dean.'

'Now you mention it, sir, I do seem to remember some of the boys whispering about nabbing someone or other,' Ken Kerrberry said. 'They were planning to hide him in the place they store the gas and oxygen cylinders.'

'Thank you.' The dean nodded briskly. 'I'll remember your helpfulness later, Mr Kerrberry.'

All six went down in the lift together.

At the door of the surgical block, the two students walked slowly away in the opposite direction towards the maternity department. Once out of sight, they broke into a run towards the empty ante-natal clinic on the ground floor. As they hurried along the corridor, banging and shouting came from the room in which Eric Cavendish was imprisoned.

'Let me out! I'm dying of cold in here. Doctor, Doctor! I'd rather die of radiation sickness than cold. At least it takes longer –'

'Relax, Mr Cavendish, relax, everything's going splendidly,' Terry shouted cheerfully through the door. He added to Ken in a whisper, 'I suppose we'd better release him?'

'You heard the dean. He'd really have it in for us.'

'The bloke himself might turn nasty.'

'But remember what Grimsdyke said. He's got a terrific sense of humour. He'll probably roar his guts out.'

'I hope so –' Terry paused, key in his hand. 'His clothes!'

'Oh, God.'

'That was your bloody stupid idea, hiding them among the patients' gear up in the ward cupboard.'

'It was your bloody stupid idea of taking them, anyway.'

'We had to be sure be didn't escape, hadn't we? In his movies, he gets out of bloody sight trickier situations than this.'

Eric Cavendish started banging on the door again. 'Get one of those trolleys – the one with the blankets,' Ken commanded.

The actor was standing in the middle of the floor, shivering and preserving his modesty behind POSTNATAL EXERCISES FOR MOTHERS.

'What's that trolley for? Where are you taking me?'

'Jump on, Mr Cavendish. No need to worry. We're just taking you up to the other decontamination room, where your clothes are waiting for you. In a few minutes you'll be able to walk out of the hospital, perfectly clean and well. We've even sent for your chauffeur to collect you.'

'Oh – thank you, Doctor,' said Eric Cavendish, calming down and climbing gratefully under the blanket.

With a sense of relief he let himself be wheeled along the corridor, through a door, across an open space, through more doors, and into a lift. He noticed that his doctors had fallen silent, and propelled him at a brisk trot. The lift stopped. They pushed him into another spacious, well-lit corridor.

'You've been a devil of a time with that patient of mine. Come along, boy, not that way, the anaesthetic room's here. Surely you've learned at least that in the hospital?'

'I recognize that voice –' Eric Cavendish raised his head. 'Well! Fancy meeting you in this charnel house.'

'My dear Cavendish, so *you're* the patient? That idiotic houseman never told me it was a private case. I didn't imagine full-time professors were allowed them, but I suppose everything has lapsed badly since my day. I shall pass the fee to Bingham, anyway. Come along, boy, push him in,' Sir Lancelot snapped to Terry, dragging the trolley into the small, cream-painted bare anaesthetic room with his own hands. 'Now let me see, Cavendish, what were you admitted here for? I must say, you never mentioned it when we were sharing a room in that quack's establishment. I hope it isn't one of those diseases people feel ashamed of?'

'I was admitted for decontamination, I guess.'

'Really? How extraordinary.' Sir Lancelot whipped off the blankets. 'Cough.'

The actor coughed.

'Again.'

Sir Lancelot looked puzzled. 'Which side is it?'

'Is what?'

'The hernia.'

'But I haven't got a hernia.'

'Come, come, man, you can't get out of an operation because your nerve fails at the last moment. Of course you've got a hernia. On the left, I think. Not a large one, but pronounced enough. Right you are. Everything's ready. I'll have it sewn up for you in no time.'

The actor sat bolt upright. 'What *is* this? You're not going to operate on *me*.'

'And why not, pray? You signed a standard consent form, I presume? It states specifically that you may possibly not have the surgeon of your choice, and that the extent of the procedure is left entirely to his skill and discretion.'

'There's nothing wrong with me,' Eric Cavendish shouted. 'And if there was, I wouldn't let you within five miles of it.'

'Now you're being insulting.'

'I'm not. I'm being sane. I remember all those spine-chilling tales you told me. About the kidney coming away in your hands. About the blood lapping over the top of your rubber operating boots. About the time you lost your half-hunter watch —'

'Come along, Cavendish, play the man! You may be the neurotic type, but you've nothing to fear —'

'I am *not* going to have an operation!'

'You are.'

'I have made my mind up.'

'And so have I. Hold him!' Sir Lancelot cried to the two students, listening to the exchange with the numb feeling of car-drivers who have precipitated a nasty accident. 'Go on, jump on him.'

Eric Cavendish leapt from the trolley. He abandoned even his blanket. He fled through the anaesthetic room doors. Outside was the matron.

He stopped short. 'Good God, Charlotte. What are you doing here?'

'Good God, Eric. But what are *you* doing here?' She looked him up and down. 'Like that?'

22

'Oh the shame!' cried the dean. 'The disgrace! The humiliation! That ghastly business of Rag Week was bad enough, capturing that poor actor and getting the hospital on the front page of every newspaper in the country. Thank God Lancelot had the wits to calm him down with an expensive dinner. I thought at the time nothing could possibly be worse. But I was wrong, wrong. Compared with this latest outrage, that was a mere April Fool's Day practical joke.'

It was the Wednesday morning of the following week. Professor Bingham, sitting in the next chair, pulled his white coat round him tightly. 'Come, Dean. Don't take it too much to heart.'

'Too much to heart? You must be mad. I'm the laughing-stock of London. Possibly of the entire medical world. You know how these disgraceful stories get about. It's really more than flesh and blood can bear.'

'In six months, everyone will have forgotten it.'

'I doubt that,' said the dean bitterly. 'Anyway, *I* shan't have forgotten it.'

'A pity, I suppose, that your own family was involved in the incident.'

'A pity? That's the most horrible part of it. A month ago – a week ago – I shouldn't have thought such a thing remotely possible. Even now, I can't honestly believe that this "incident" – as you somewhat ridiculously term the greatest disaster of my life since failing my surgery finals – has actually happened.'

'It can hardly be held against *your* reputation, surely?'

'Of course it can. These things rub off.' He shook his head miserably. 'You don't understand how careful I must be, keeping my nose clean for a month or so. As it is, I very much doubt if I shall ever see a knight –'

'Yes?'

'If I shall ever see a night fall again.'

'I say, you're not going to commit suicide, are you?' asked Bingham in alarm. 'It can't be quite as bad as that.'

'That's not what I mean at all. I mean…that is…oh, I don't know what I mean,' the dean ended hopelessly.

The pair were alone in the big, oblong, dark-panelled committee room at St Swithin's, its walls decorated with portraits of consultant physicians and surgeons who had followed their patients into eternity. In the centre was a long, stout-legged table at which the dean and the professor sat. Its well-polished surface was covered with sheets of pink blotting-paper, duplicated pages of typescript, and open reference-books. The full disciplinary committee of the hospital had just met.

This fearsome body, with which the dean had threatened Terry Summerbee, convened only rarely to pronounce on graver misdemeanours by the hospital students or staff. It consisted of senior consultants, and took itself most seriously. Indeed, it could in a bad mood make the Star Chamber look as harmless as a rent tribunal.

The dean sat silently for a few moments, bouncing on the edge of his chair. He was naturally a member of the committee, but with a short, dignified speech he had withdrawn from the morning's proceedings. He had waited outside, pacing up and down, to appear only after the verdict had been pronounced.

This was necessary because the unfortunate delinquent had been his own son.

'To think – that George actually committed forgery.'

'But only of your own signature.'

'That's even worse, when he used it to gain admission to the Ministry building. I still can't imagine how he managed to hide himself there until morning.'

'In the lavatory.'

'What an uncomfortable place to pass a night. Of course, he told me some cock-and-bull story about emergency work at St Swithin's, which being a trusting and considerate father I believed implicitly. Then for him to be discovered…in the morning…in the Minister's own room…by the Minister himself…under the Minister's own desk…'

'But is that really so terrible? These days, nowhere is sacred. The sit-in has become a form of student protest so conventional as to be positively boring.'

'Yes, but not in the nude.'

'Possibly.'

'Thank God the quality of mercy was not strained and all's well that ends well,' the dean said confusedly.

'We'd really no alternative to leniency. After all, everyone on the committee knew George to be a young man of the highest character and strictest up-bringing. The point was made by several members. It was all so out of character, we could only ascribe it to some acute psychological upset. Hysteria, hypomania, something like that. He'll attend the psychiatric department for a while, and afterwards he can get on with his work as if nothing had happened. Perhaps it was the strain of study? Overwork?' Bingham gave a thin smile. 'I say, Dean, you do push your children hard, eh?'

'But I still can't for the life of me think how this fantastic idea got into George's head.'

'In a way, it was a rather humorous one.'

'That's what Lancelot says. He's been laughing his head off. Like a hyena. God! I wish the bloody man would leave us in peace.'

'At least you'll get rid of him for his honeymoon the day after tomorrow.'

'Yes, five days in Brighton. Then he's coming back to live in that block of new flats opposite my house, which has ruined my view of the park, anyway.'

'Pity he wouldn't go on the cruise.'

'You know whose fault that is. Really, Bingham. Surely you can give him his money back? After all, it's not a fortune as such things go. Not compared with our expectations from the Blaydon Trust.'

'Expectations! The Blaydon gift is not signed, sealed, and delivered. Sir Lancelot's is in the bank.'

'A mere administrative detail. You could easily afford to disgorge. He might at least disappear with his bride to Wales. I happen to know he's itching to start trout fishing, now the season's open.'

'It's a matter of principle.'

'I wish you wouldn't be so smug, Bingham.' The dean looked offended. 'You sometimes make the rest of us feel like a bunch of train robbers.'

'Perhaps I have reason to be smug?'

'That's worse. Now you're smug about being smug – '

Bingham laid a hand on his arm. 'I say, you *are* becoming over-excited. It can't be doing much good to your systolic pressure. Just relax a minute, while I tell you exactly what I'm feeling smug about. You may find it extremely interesting.'

The dean looked puzzled. 'Well, make it brief. I want my lunch.'

'Isn't it strange how unlikely events can sometimes have even more unlikely consequences? The spore of penicillin mould which blew through the window of Fleming's laboratory at St Mary's – '

'Come on, man!'

'I mean, your son's little aberration could prove a great benefit to us all.'

'What the hell are you getting at?'

Professor Bingham reached for a large, ancient leather-bound book on the middle of the committee-table. 'You know what this is? The minute-book of the full disciplinary committee.' He ran his hand fondly over its glossy cover. 'It seldom sees the light of day. It was only with difficulty that, as the committee's secretary, I managed to find it before the present meeting. It was tucked away among piles of bound surgical reports from Victorian days. An unlikely place. Perhaps someone had been hoping to hide it.'

'Look here, Bingham, what *are* you trying to say? I'm hungry.'

'I am trying to say – in short – that I can guarantee Sir Lancelot will leave for his honeymoon on Friday and never show his face in St Swithin's, or even London, for the rest of his life.'

23

While the dean sat with Professor Bingham in the committee room at St Swithin's, his daughter Muriel was hurrying away from a bus stop up the steep pavements of Highgate Hill. Halfway along she turned into a street of small shops which until recently had been selling fish and chips and newspapers, but with the rediscovery of the area as amusingly original to live in were taken over by the purveyors of more fashionable things. Muriel suddenly stopped. She hitched up her skirt until it barely covered her thighs. She looked down approvingly. Her legs were really quite good. She wondered desperately if Albert would notice them.

Muriel pushed open the shop door. 'Hello!' she cried joyfully. 'I'm here.'

'Hello, then.'

Albert appeared from the dim interior of his boutique into the light of day, like some round and shaggy animal emerging from its den. The object of Muriel's passion was a young man five feet high and almost two across. It was difficult to know what he looked like, the unclothed parts of him being largely invisible under a thick matting of hair. The hair on his head fell to his shoulders. His thick frizzy ginger sideboards suggested the rope fenders of a ship. The moustache covering his upper lip changed direction abruptly at the corner of his mouth and ran downwards towards his chin. Massive eyebrows thatched his bulging eyes, and a small pointed beard somehow kept its identity in the general growth. He was dressed with fashionable scruffiness in jeans and a jacket of khaki drill.

'Well, then,' he repeated.

Muriel threw her arms round him, and finding a reasonably bare area gave it a kiss. 'Aren't you pleased to see me?'

'Course.'

'Albert, my darling! It's been terrible this week, not meeting you even once.'

'Has it, then?'

'You got my letter?'

'Yes.'

Muriel couldn't suppress her trembling. He was so more experienced, so more worldly then herself she continually feared he must find her dull. In fact, he treated the world – which he divided simply into customers, birds, and people – with an off-handedness he thought as fashionable as his clothes.

'Well, then,' he said.

'Aren't you going to kiss me?'

'I might.'

She was thrilled as he pressed his lips hard on hers, though she felt somewhere in her mind it was like being slapped in the face with a damp doormat. She broke away, looking round guiltily. In her excitement, she hadn't cared if there were customers about. But the boutique was in its usual state of emptiness. It was a tiny slot-like place, filled with a collection of objects which had in common only that they were old, covered with dust, and slightly broken. In summer, Albert managed to sell a few of these to tourists, who found a strange happiness in decorating distant homes with horse-brasses or cockle-plates, or even flag-emblazoned admirals' chamber-pots. In the days before boutiques, the establishment would have traded under the good honest name of a junk shop.

'Well, Albert, my sweet. Where are you taking me to lunch?' He scratched his side-whiskers. 'Oh, Albert! Don't say you've forgotten.'

'Perhaps I have.'

'Well, here I am, so let's go, anyway,' she said brightly.

'Pub do you?'

She was disappointed. She had been anticipating a pleasant meal in some quiet and possibly romantic restaurant. But she gave another smile. 'You know I'd go anywhere with you, Albert my love.'

'I'd better lock the place up properly. Lot of criminals about these days.'

He shot the bolts of the back door thoughtfully. He wondered exactly how he had got mixed up with this peculiar virgin. Perhaps he had been more drunk than he had imagined at that party in the student's flat. Or perhaps it was the medical bit about her which attracted him. He wondered if he harboured some mild peculiarity about female doctors, like a friend of his who was continually getting himself in trouble with policewomen.

They went into a small public house with decorative frosted-glass windows, just across the road. Albert directed her to the public bar, where he bought her a light ale and a ham roll.

'Albert,' she announced. 'I've something important to tell you.'

'Oh, yes?'

'You see, I…I seem to have so little to offer you. So I decided that…instead…I'd like to help you in your work.'

'Serve in the shop, then?'

'Well, not actually that. I've my classes at St Swithin's. Though I should love to really, it must be wonderful handling all those lovely and precious things. But I thought I might be able to help you with introductions to important customers.'

Albert looked more interested. He was an enterprising young man, with an admirable sharpness for such opportunities as presented themselves in his somewhat dreary life.

She felt in her handbag and handed him a visiting card. He put down his pint and studied it carefully. It was printed:

Dr Lionel Lychfleld, DSc, MD, FRCP
164 Grace Gardens,
NW1
01-467 3128

'Might be useful.' He turned it over slowly. 'Ta.'

'You could show it to people, you see,' she said a little breathlessly. 'And they'd think he'd sent you, on a personal recommendation, to sell them antiques.'

'They might not believe me.'

'Why shouldn't they?'

'Well... ' He scratched himself again. 'Look, love. It would be better if he'd put a signed message on it.'

'I don't think I could persuade him to do that,' she said doubtfully.

'Who's got to persuade anyone?' He laughed. 'You do it.'

'Oh...but that *would* be rather naughty of me, wouldn't it?'

He picked up his pint. 'What's it matter, if no one finds out?'

Muriel took out her ball-point. She wrote on the card, *This is to introduce Mr Albert Duttle (antique specialist) who is most reliable. L Lychfield.*

'There you are.' She handed it back delightedly. The deed once done, she had only to enjoy his appreciation.

'Ta,' he said, slipping the card into the back pocket of his jeans.

'Who are you going to try it on, Albert dear?'

'That's the point, innit? Who d'you know interested in buying high-class antiques?'

'Daddy's and mummy's friends are no use, because of course they'd ring him up and everything would come to light. So would all the consultants at the hospital.' She sipped her light ale thoughtfully. 'I know! *Much* better.' She came so near him she was in danger of getting a mouthful of hair. She whispered, 'Have you heard of someone called Lady Blaydon?'

'Can't say I have.'

'Well, daddy has been mixed up with her lawyers and people over the past few months. She's been giving a lot of money to the hospital.'

'She's loaded?'

Muriel nodded eagerly. 'Daddy says she's filthy rich. I heard she lives in those huge flats overlooking St James's Park. My father doesn't actually know her, so she'd just think he was one of your satisfied customers. You could go on your motor-bike and see if she's interested in buying anything. If she isn't there's no harm done, is there?'

'Maybe.' He considered for some moments. 'It's nice to do business with the better class of person. They're more appreciative of good stuff. Ta.' He added condescendingly, 'Care for another light?'

24

That night the dean dreamt that the Queen on her flag-decked dais was executing him again. He woke sweating, relieved that it was but a fantasy. He glanced at his bedside clock, and saw that it was already past seven in the morning. Then a warm feeling grew upon him. This particular day was going to be one of the most satisfying of his life.

The dean usually made a brisk toilet, anxious to be out of the house and away to the hospital. He had been even quicker during the last week in an attempt to be off before Sir Lancelot got down to breakfast. Approaching marriage, far from mellowing the surgeon's mood, seemed to put him in an increasingly filthy temper. But that morning the dean tarried in the bath and fiddled with his clothes, seeing his wife go downstairs first. He wanted to be completely sure of finding himself alone after breakfast with his guest.

By the time the dean reached the table, Josephine had already snatched a cup of coffee and hurried to Bond Street for a final fitting of the dress she had bought for the following day's wedding. Muriel rose and said she had a patient to examine before the teaching-round. George alone sat yawning over his cornflakes. The boy always seems so tired these mornings, the dean thought testily. Perhaps he ought to have some treatment for it.

There was only one letter beside his plate. It was from the senior consultant psychiatrist at St Swithin's.

The dean read it, with a grunt. 'You seem to have impressed the psychiatry people at St Swithin's at your consultation yesterday afternoon.'

George looked at him silently. Since the incident of the Minister's desk he had been too terrified to speak to his father at all. 'Impressed them?'

'Yes. That you are mentally unsuited to the occupation of medicine.'

A slow smile spread over George's face.

'They go further. They imply that you are mentally unsuited for any occupation whatsoever.' He tossed the letter down. 'Well, if you want to give it up, you may as well, I suppose. Even though I wouldn't take the word of a psychiatrist on the suitability of a fish to water. You represent a great waste of time and money, but as you have little idea of the value of either I suppose that won't trouble your conscience.'

'But Dad –'

The dean stopped him. 'I don't want another word about it. It is a most painful subject to me. Once we have Sir Lancelot out of the way, we can settle down to discuss your career. Perhaps you would do well to emigrate.'

George spooned the rest of the cornflakes into his mouth and scurried away. The dean picked up the morning paper. Inga came in silently to clear the dirty dishes. Miss MacNish, the dean knew, had gone to have her hair done for the wedding. They would be undisturbed. The scene was set, the drama could begin.

'Morning, Dean.' Sir Lancelot appeared and sat at the table. 'Sling us the bit of the paper with the crossword, will you? I rather like having a stab at it over breakfast.'

The dean stared at him coldly. He ran his tongue over his lips. 'It might interest you to know, Lancelot, that it is one of the remaining small pleasures of my busy and overtaxed life also to have a stab at the crossword over breakfast. I only manage to see my newspaper at all because I specifically ordered Miss MacNish shortly after your arrival *not* to send it directly to your bedroom with your morning tea.'

Sir Lancelot sniffed. 'I've worse things to worry about, I suppose.' He poured himself some coffee. 'Slacking this morning, I see? You're usually at the hospital by now.'

'I am not slacking. I was waiting specifically until you came down.'

'Civil of you, but as a matter of fact I really prefer solitude for this particular meal.'

'I have something to say which I fear will cause you considerable dismay.'

'You're not on about that bloody electric blanket again, are you?'

'Lancelot, when you leave this house tomorrow morning for the registry office, you will be leaving it for good. On that, I think we are fully agreed. But you will be leaving St Swithin's for good, too.'

Sir Lancelot glared. 'What's all this? Are you ordering me about, you little hearthrug Napoleon?'

'I was intending to put an unpleasant matter to you as kindly as possible. If you persist in using such terms, I shall employ less finesse.'

'Dean, do shut up and ring the bell for my eggs and bacon.'

'I think you would prefer us to have no audience. Lancelot, will you turn your mind back to the occasion of Thursday, June the twenty-fifth, 1953? That was Coronation year.'

Sir Lancelot pondered for some time. 'It was the first day of the Lord's Test against the Australians under Hassett, the season we got the Ashes back by winning the final game at the Oval —'

'I'm not asking about trivia,' snapped the dean. 'I should have imagined the date was stamped indelibly on your memory. It was that of a meeting of the full disciplinary committee at the hospital.'

'H'm,' said Sir Lancelot.

The dean picked up a butter-knife and started tapping the dish to emphasize his points.

'That June day you were still Mr Spratt, a junior consultant on the staff of St Swithin's. Though you perhaps did not realize it, you stood on the threshold of your greatest days as a surgeon — which, I freely and gladly admit, brought immense benefit to mankind and considerable renown to the hospital.'

'H'm,' repeated Sir Lancelot.

'You appeared before the committee in rather peculiar circumstances.' The dean tapped louder. 'In the first place, it was convened with a bare quorum, only three members. Most irregular. The meeting was at an unusual time — nine in the evening, when few consultants could have been in the hospital. And of those three committee members, all now unhappily dead, two were consultant physicians related to your family by marriage. The chairman was the retiring senior surgeon, who was your uncle. Odd.'

'I do wish you'd stop playing "God Save the Queen" on that ruddy butter-dish.'

The dean abruptly dropped the knife. 'Furthermore, Lancelot, in a most mysterious manner the relevant pages of the minute-book became gummed together.'

'Nothing mysterious about it whatever. I gummed them.'

'With the aid of a scalpel, the story of the meeting is now revealed. The proceedings seem to have been ridiculously brief and laughably lenient. A reprimand, I recall, was the only punishment. Everything was conducted with discretion, even delicacy. The lady in question was referred to throughout simply as "Mrs X". I shall not press you who the unfortunate female was –'

'You'd damn well better not, and she was *not* unfortunate.'

'Nevertheless, Lancelot, you outraged decency by taking her away for the weekend. To France. To Le Touquet. I must say, you do seem to enjoy making history repeat itself.'

'Well? What great harm was there in that, as you pointed out in your office? Even if I have done it twice in my life.'

'With a difference. On the recent occasion, the lady who accompanied you is tomorrow to become your wife. Even the narrowest moralist would strain himself objecting to that. But on the earlier expedition the lady already had a husband.'

'They were joined only formally.'

'That is absolutely nothing to do with it. Luckily for you, the husband did not indeed seem particularly affronted. He simply complained to the hospital, and left St Swithin's to take the matter further if they thought fit.'

'I don't see what business it was of the hospital's, anyway.'

Picking up the knife again, the dean gave the butter-dish a decisive tap. 'You seem to have forgotten with the passage of time that the lady in question was also one of your patients. A few weeks previously you had removed her appendix in the private block.'

'H'm,' said Sir Lancelot again.

'Of course, I don't really believe that the General Medical Council would feel necessarily obliged to act at this stage – as it most certainly would have done, had the facts come to its notice at the time.'

'Why not, for God's sake? It isn't exactly prehistoric.'

'Because now you are retired from practice,' the dean emphasized. 'Completely retired. You do not operate. You do not see a single patient. You do not even appear inside the walls of St Swithin's. You are *absolutely retired*.'

'H'm.'

'And anyway, the gossip alone, if it got about, would not be a nice thing for a man of the integrity, the devotion to duty, the status – and, if I may add, the arrogance, stubbornness and intolerance – of yourself.'

Sir Lancelot gave a sigh. 'Blackmail?'

'That is not the word which I should use. But I suppose it is,' the dean added cheerfully.

There was a pause. 'All right. I'll get out. I'll take Tottie and keep out of your hair.'

'Very wise of you indeed, I think.'

'You mentioned a while ago about a free world cruise –'

'That offer is now closed,' said the dean firmly.

'We'll go from honeymoon back to Wales, I suppose,' Sir Lancelot said gloomily. 'At least I shall be able to get some fishing.'

The dean rose. 'Now I must be about my duties. This has been painful for me, Lancelot, very painful. I will bid you good morning. Tomorrow it will be good-bye.'

'There's just one thing, Dean.'

'Yes?'

'If you breathe one word about that affair to anyone, I really believe I shall slit your blasted throat with a bone-saw.'

The dean looked hurt. 'Come, Lancelot. Surely you can trust my discretion? After all, we're lifelong friends, aren't we?'

25

Everyone in the dean's household was up early the next day, except Sir Lancelot. The dean himself appeared in his best suit, rubbing his hands and beaming at a disruption which, on normal mornings, would have incited outbursts comparable to *King Lear*. He had grudgingly agreed some days before to the wedding-reception being held in his home – Sir Lancelot disliked hotels, and anyway thought it a neat way to keep down the onlookers. Miss MacNish and Josephine had been almost continually in the kitchen for forty-eight hours, and now the large dining-room was emptied of its normal furniture to contain a pair of long tables covered with stiff white cloths. One bore various succulent canapés and a small wedding cake, the other glasses for champagne. Breakfast for himself, the dean saw, would be a cup of coffee in the kitchen or nothing at all. But he didn't care. That morning Sir Lancelot was going. For good.

'Nothing like a wedding for setting the womenfolk in a twitter,' he remarked to Josephine, giving the dining-room a genial glance. 'Even though the bridegroom is of retirement age and the bride old enough to know better. What a curiously standardized form of human nourishment these little cocktail things are,' he added, picking up a square of toast with a slice of egg and two tips of asparagus on it. 'One gets exactly the same at receptions in New York or Buenos Aires or Melbourne or Tokyo.' He swallowed it. 'I must write a letter to *The Times* about that some day.'

'Lionel!' exclaimed his wife excitedly. 'I've got some – oh, please don't eat any more of those canapés, we've hardly enough to go round as it is – I've got some simply wonderful news.'

'You've heard? Yes, it's splendid, isn't it?'

'Then *you've* heard? And you agree?'

'Of course I agree. I've been working towards that precise end for weeks.'

'*Have* you? That's funny. I rather sensed you disapproved of the whole idea.'

'What on earth put that in your head? We shall get a little peace at last when he's left our family circle.'

'Of course, he's a bit noisy sometimes. But we shall miss him dreadfully, of course.'

'Miss him? Oh, yes! like the garbage when the dustmen empty it on Monday mornings.'

'Lionel! What a – *please* don't eat any more of those – what a way to talk about your own son.'

'I didn't even mention my own son,' he told her irritably. 'I mean Lancelot.'

'You seem absolutely obsessed with Lancelot. Do please listen to me for a moment. They want to get married.'

'Of course they do. What do you imagine this banquet is for?'

'I mean George wants to marry Inga.'

'Does he indeed? We'll soon see about that. What's the little fool going to live on? He'll not have a penny from me. And he won't get very fat on that drivel he writes for television. He'll go on the buses, I presume. I shouldn't think even Inga will stand for that.'

'Why are you always so horrible about little Inga?'

'Well, she can't expect much. She told me her father was a match-seller in Stockholm. Almost a beggar, I suppose.'

'I do wish you'd make allowance for the poor girl's English. He sells his Swedish matches by the hundred million. Every day.'

'Oh, really?'

'And there's another point. Inga won't look at him unless he sticks to medicine. She's got sense, you see. She wants him to have a nice steady job.' Josephine laughed. 'She'd make a wonderful doctor's wife. She's even antiseptic to look at, isn't she?'

The newly-engaged pair, listening outside, felt it the moment to enter the dining-room, holding hands and looking sheepish.

'Then I'm delighted,' the dean decided. In his mood that morning he could have been delighted had his son announced he was going to marry Sarah Gamp. 'Yes, you have my blessing, as they used to say in the days when children took parents into their confidence about such things. Well, well! Fancy you getting married, George. I never credited you with the initiative. Now you are taking unto yourself a wife, you must steady up, take a serious and sober view of life. There's nothing frivolous or amusing about marriage, you know.'

'Yes, Dad. So you say.'

'I must confess, I have often wished you possessed some of the commonsense and social responsibility shown by your sister Muriel – '

Miss MacNish appeared in the room. 'Doctor, three policemen have just arrived.'

'Policemen? I didn't send for any policemen. To control the traffic outside, I suppose. Must be Lancelot's doing. Gross extravagance. You don't get them free, you know, you have to pay. Tell them to go away.'

'I did, Doctor. But they won't.'

'What impertinence. Say we don't want their services, it was all a mistake. I shall write to Scotland Yard about it.'

'They have a search warrant, Doctor.'

The dean went rigid. 'Search warrant? But there must be some mistake…'

'You'd better ask them in and get it over. Before Lancelot gets down,' said Josephine grimly.

'Yes, yes, show them in,' said the dean, nervously picking up a triangle of smoked salmon on brown bread and swallowing it.

There were two policemen in uniform, politely removing their helmets. The other was a thick-set young man in plain clothes.

'Afraid we've disrupted a party, sir,' he said cheerfully, waving an identity card in the dean's direction.

'But this…this is a gross violation of the liberty of the subject.'

'I know how you feel, sir. We won't keep you long. I'd like a word with Miss Muriel Lychfield, of this address.'

'My daughter? But why?'

'I have a warrant for her arrest, sir.'

'Oh!' cried Josephine.

'What is happening?' Inga asked George nervously. 'Will they now beat-up your father?'

Muriel at that moment came through the door with a tray of asparagus in brown-bread overcoats.

'They've come to take you off to prison,' said the dean.

She dropped the tray. She clapped her hands over her mouth. The detective drew from his raincoat pocket a small silver object shaped like an elephant. 'This your property, miss?' She could say nothing. He turned to the dean. 'Or yours, sir?'

'Never seen it before in my life. I don't even know what it is.'

'It's a silver sugar caster, of distinctive shape.' The detective turned it over. 'Quite thoughtfully pretty really. I'm rather interested in antiques. We get quite a variety through our hands, as you'd expect, one way and another.'

'*What* is this all about?' the dean demanded.

'Daddy,' said Muriel. 'I've been a fool.'

'Will you answer a few questions first, sir?'

'Anything you like.' The dean clasped his forehead. 'My God! My knight—'

'Yes?'

'My — "my nightshirt". It's an expression. I use it sometimes.'

The detective looked at him curiously. 'We received a complaint last night from a Lady Blaydon — are you all right, sir?'

'Yes, yes. A little dizzy.'

'Should I call a doctor?'

'I am one, damn it.'

'Sorry, sir. Just forgetting for the moment. Lady Blaydon stated that a man named Albert Duttle called at her flat yesterday afternoon on the pretext of selling antiques. When he left, this property was missing.'

'Albert Duttle? Never heard of him.'

'Oh, Daddy!' said Muriel. 'I *have* been a fool.'

'But he knows your daughter, sir.'

'Muriel! It can't be? Surely not?'

'Oh, Daddy! I've been a *bloody* fool.'

151

'Everyone's gone mad.' The dean leant against the wall. Josephine put her arm round him. 'Perhaps I'm dreaming it? Yes, I'm dreaming it. The Queen's going to cut my head off.'

The detective looked puzzled. 'It's a serious offence, sir, but not as serious as that.'

'But how did our daughter get mixed up in all this?' asked Josephine.

'We easily traced Duttle to a crummy little antique shop he runs. He's one of our regulars. We found the missing property. It seems your daughter had conspired with him in stealing it.' The detective took a manila envelope from his inside pocket. Extracting a visiting card, he handed it silently to the dean.

'That's my card, all right. Undeniably. But I certainly never wrote *that*. It isn't my writing. It —' He looked in alarm at Muriel.

'Oh, Daddy! I've been such a bloody *awful* fool.'

'Looks like a clear case,' the detective said with satisfaction. 'I expect we'll have you, too, Doctor. Accessory before the fact.'

The dean started waving his arms about. 'All right. Arrest me. Arrest us all. Imprison and disgrace the lot of us. Kick me into the gutter. Only someone tell me one thing. Why has a sensible level-headed girl like my daughter suddenly started consorting with the lowest criminals?'

'It was Sir Lancelot,' said Muriel. 'He said I should help Albert in his work. I stayed away from the hospital one morning specially to ask his advice. It was the day he told George to hide naked under the Minister's desk.'

The dean was vaguely aware of a young man pushing into the room.

'It was my fault,' announced the newcomer. 'I accept all blame. It was my idea to go ahead with the plot, and I'm prepared to take the consequences.'

The dean stared. 'You're not Duttle. You're Summerbee.' A thought struck him. 'Or do you work under an alias?'

'I didn't really come to confess, sir. But as the police are involved, I'm prepared to give myself up.'

'But you're always taking the bloody blame, damn it. What are you, boy? Some kind of masochist?'

'About the kidnapping, sir.'

'Kidnapping?' The detective looked up.

'Also, sir, I want to tell you this – the way you treat your daughter would make a Victorian novel look like *Candy*. And furthermore, I intend to put a stop to it by taking her off to live with me. But I'll marry her first, if she really wants to.'

'Terry, darling!' They grabbed each other. 'How could I have been so *blind*? I was mad, mad! Terry, how I love you!'

The dean reached out a shaking hand for an anchovy on a strip of toast, and munched it with an abstracted air. 'I shall kill myself,' he muttered. 'Bingham can have the bits.'

'Hello! The party started already? You might at least have held your horses till the ceremony was over, Dean. What have you got the house full of policemen for? If you imagine there's valuable wedding presents to guard, I'm afraid everyone will be sadly mistaken. No breakfast, I suppose? Then I fancy I'll settle for a glass of champagne. George, be a good fellow and open a bottle in the ice-bucket. You know how, I presume, without drowning the lot of us? I say, that's Sergeant Morgan-Jones, isn't it? Quite forgot you were in the plain-clothes branch. How's the old hernia?'

'Fine, Sir Lancelot. Never a moment's trouble since you fixed it at St Swithin's.'

'Must have been about the last case before I retired. Still playing rugger?'

'Putting on a bit of weight now, I'm afraid, sir.'

'Damn good three-quarter you were for the Metropolitan Police. Shocking booze-up we had when you gave the St Swithin's fifteen a hiding that season, wasn't it? How on earth do you manage to get back from the ground these days of the breathalyser? Borrow a black maria for the evening, I suppose –'

'Lancelot,' croaked the dean. 'Help me.'

'I say, Dean, you don't look very well. That electric blanket been playing you up, or something?'

'Something awful has happened. I face the prospect of a criminal charge.'

'Really? Well, that's not a nice thing for a man of the integrity, the devotion to duty, the position – and, if I may add, the miserliness, deviousness and selfishness – of yourself.'

'You *must* help me.'

'Not much time, really. In an hour I'm getting married. Then I'm on my honeymoon and then I'm retiring to Wales. But do send me a postcard to say how the trial turns out.'

'Lancelot, you must *not* leave London. Only you can save me.'

'Damnation, man, do you want to exile me or keep us both on as lodgers? At least make up your mind.' He took a glass of champagne from George. 'Good morning, Grimsdyke,' he added genially as the young doctor came in, holding Stella by the hand. 'To what do I – or rather the dean – owe this unexpected visit?'

'We're getting married, sir, at the same registry office. In fact, we're next on the bill to you. I thought it would be a bit of a laugh if we all went along together.'

'A very pleasant idea. Have some champagne. The rest of you look as though you could do with a glass, too. Not you and your men, I suppose, Sergeant, either on duty or in training? George, you'd better open another bottle. My dear Tottie, how nice to see you. Though shouldn't I by rights only set eyes on you at the registry office? Otherwise it's seven years' bad luck, or something, I believe.'

'Lancelot.' She ignored everyone in the room. 'I've got to speak to you. In private.'

'Then let's step into the dean's study next door. It's getting horribly crowded in here, anyway. Do you mind if I bring my champagne?'

They went into the small study next door. 'Lancelot –'

'You look awfully smart, Tottie. Wedding-gear suits you.'

'That's the point, Lancelot. There isn't going to be a wedding.'

'Oh, really?'

'Oh, Lancelot!' She started to cry. 'How can I do this to you?'

'Come, come.' He offered his red-and-white handkerchief. 'Tell me the trouble. Are you married already, or somesuch?'

'Almost.' She shook her head miserably. 'You know when I left St Swithin's for America? I ended up working in an expensive private clinic in Los Angeles. It was there I met Eric Cavendish, as a patient.'

'You told me this when we all three had dinner after that students' prank.'

'But what I didn't tell you was that we lived together afterwards.'

'I see.'

'Until we had a row, and I went back to nursing.'

'I see.'

'The row was about women. Young women. Very young women. Eric has a sort of kink about them. I don't know what the psychologists call it, a Lolita complex or something. I managed to restrain him. *Only* I managed to restrain him. Once he was loose from me, he got into all sorts of trouble. There's no knowing where it might end.'

'I see.'

They stood looking at each other.

'Now his wife's divorced him at last, I want to marry him, Lancelot.'

'Forgive me for putting it this way, Tottie, but to become a sort of psychiatric nurse-cum-wardress? It doesn't sound a great deal of fun.'

'No, Eric's changing. I think he only chases girls to prove his virility. Surely *I* could do that for him.'

'I'm quite certain you could.'

'And I love him. I always did. All the time, even when I was back at St Swithin's trying to forget everything.'

'It would be excessively churlish of me to stand in your way.'

'Lancelot, you're wonderful.'

'Oh, come. An ordinary sort, really. But I do have my principles.'

'How can I possibly repay you?'

'Perhaps you have already?' He smiled. 'That was a delightful week in Le Touquet.'

She smiled too. 'We had fun, didn't we? Even dancing! That tune you made them play – what was it? From the musical, *Guys and Dolls* – I remember, "I've Never Been In Love Before".'

'A sentimental air.'

'Lancelot – whatever happens...whatever you may think of me...please believe me when I thank you for...perhaps the most charming and most thrilling week of my whole life.'

'I am touched.'

'Now perhaps I'd better simply disappear. Eric has his car waiting. Neither you nor anyone in the hospital will ever set eyes on me again.'

Sir Lancelot bent over to kiss her. Then she turned and hurried out of the house.

He returned to the dining-room. 'More champagne. Come on, George, jump to it. You're not opening bottles like a St Swithin's student at all.'

'What is it, Lancelot?' asked Josephine. 'Some wonderful piece of news?'

'Yes. The wedding's off.'

'Lancelot,' cried the dean, who had not seemed to hear. 'I've had time to collect my thoughts. I must talk to you. Come into my study at once.'

'My dear Dean, I cannot run some sort of shuttle service.'

'I implore you.'

'Oh, very well.' The surgeon reopened the door. 'What are you doing, dressed up like that?' he demanded of a figure in a *dhoti* in the hall.

'But I'm Godfri. I'm taking the wedding photographs. The bride commissioned me.'

'They're all grouped in the room,' Sir Lancelot told him. 'Just go in with that little camera of yours and start shooting.'

'Lancelot —' The dean shut the study door behind him. 'Bingham told me you know Lady Blaydon personally.'

'I'm acquainted with her, yes. I do wish you'd stop waving that sausage roll at me.'

'Oh. Yes.' The dean stared in surprise, and threw it into the wastepaper basket. 'Can't you see her? As an intermediary? Use whatever influence you have? Ask her to withdraw the charge against this terrible man Muriel was mixed with? I'm sure she'd do that, anyway. But about the money she promised the hospital from the Blaydon Trust —'

'You haven't a chance in hell of that. She hates being made a fool of.'

'You're my only hope, Lancelot. The hospital's only hope —'

'You're not all that broke. Bingham's still got my fifty thousand.'

'A mere drop in the ocean compared with the Blaydon bequest —' The dean snatched a cheque book from the desk and scribbled. 'There! It's on the St Swithin's account. Every penny returned to you.'

Sir Lancelot thoughtfully folded the slip of paper and tucked it in his pocket. 'I don't see why I should let that influence me, as it's mine anyway.'

'Lancelot, in the name of our lifelong friendship in our mutual profession —'

'From which you cheerfully threatened to get me kicked out.'

'Lionel, go outside at once.' Josephine appeared in the study. 'Go on. I want to speak to Lancelot alone.'

Looking miserably from one to the other, the dean obeyed.

'Lancelot.' She calmed herself. 'I must tell you a secret. Lionel is up for a knighthood.'

'Knew that before he did, m'dear. The Minister fishes my salmon water in Wales. I put in a good word for him, as it happened.'

'Oh, Lancelot! How kind-hearted you are underneath.'

He stroked his beard. 'I have my softer moments.'

'But this morning his chances of honours have been shattered.'

'Well, they haven't been improved much, I agree. Getting someone to nick the silver from the hospital's prize benefactress.'

'But Lionel said you actually knew Lady Blaydon. Couldn't you see her? I implore you, from the bottom of my heart.'

'Very well,' Sir Lancelot decided. 'As it's you who asks, m'dear.'

'Oh, Lancelot! You are a sweet man!'

He patted her cheek. 'And if all the women in the world wore as well as you, Josephine, no one would give a glance at those skinny little chits in short skirts and dirty feet. I'll slip out. Ring her flat to say I'm coming. Tell your husband to keep those policemen entertained with light conversation until I get back.'

26

'But Lancelot, of course it was all a stupid mistake. What a silly billy I was! I should never have rung the police in the first place. Though I was terribly, terribly fond of that dear little sugar caster. And you know how much burglary there is in London these days, *honestly*, they break in and they take everything, absolutely *everything*, they'd strip the paper off the walls if only they had the time.'

Lady Blaydon, a long-legged redhead, leant back on the sofa in her flat with a gin-and-tonic and lit another cigarette.

'My dear little Puddy Tat —'

. She smiled fondly. 'No one's called me that for years. My husband never did, not once in his life.'

'I hope this incident will make no difference to your generosity over the new block of St Swithin's? It is a scheme dear to the heart of all of us, you know. Particularly to myself.'

'Of course not! St Swithin's is very, very dear to *my* heart.'

Sir Lancelot chuckled. 'It was the second week in May, 1953, if I recall? In Coronation year.'

'Yes! Le Touquet was *so* delightful. We had such *fun* in those days, didn't we? We even danced! I'll always remember the tune, it was out of that musical *Guys and Dolls* — "I've Never Been In Love Before".'

'I also recall that your husband was not quite so compliant as you led me to expect, Puddy Tat.'

She made a little gesture. 'Oh, he'd had a bad week at the races. He'd already lost interest in me. Though on the whole, our marriage was successful — he got the money and I got the title.'

'And you never married again.'

'I've never had time, darling, between boy friends.' An idea struck her. 'Would you like to see that lovely scar you made?'

Sir Lancelot rose. 'I must go.'

'So soon?'

'I have several people to put out of their misery. Then I must set off for my house in Wales, if I want to fish the evening rise.'

'But why don't you stay in London? It's so exciting these days.'

'Too exciting for an old man like me.'

'Old? Of course not, darling. You're exactly the man you were.'

'You tempt me very much, dear Puddy Tat, to try to demonstrate the fact.' He leant over and kissed her. 'These meetings can take terrible toll of the emotions. I fancy mine need a nice long spell of quiet recuperation in the country. Perhaps for several years.'

It was early that afternoon when Sir Lancelot left. The dean stayed away from the hospital specially to see him off. He stood with Josephine at the door of his house, while Miss MacNish helped load cases into the Rolls. As Sir Lancelot climbed into the driving-seat, the surgeon noticed she was weeping.

'I found this the other day — at the bottom of my trunk.' The housekeeper pressed into his hand a small blue-and-white china ashtray. He saw it was inscribed, *Un Cadeau du Touquet*.

'I haven't forgotten,' she smiled through the tears. 'That third week in May, in 1953. Coronation year. The first time I'd gone abroad in my life! What was that tune they played? I still hear it sometimes on the radio. "I've Never Been in Love Before" — out of one of those musical shows, *Guys and Dolls*. And to imagine! I was a young lassie just down from Aberdeen, opening the door and answering the telephone at your consulting-rooms in Harley Street.'

Sir Lancelot patted her cheek. 'I, too, shall never forget that spring in Le Touquet. And believe me, my dear, you honestly haven't changed a bit.'

He waved. They all shouted good-bye. He touched the accelerator. He drove off westward. At the first traffic-lights he sat deep in thought. 'Damn good receptionist that girl was, too,' he reflected.

As the dean shut the front door he declared to his wife, 'How I've misjudged that man all my life.'

'So many people have, dear.'

'Of course, he's got a crusty exterior. But underneath his heart is gold, pure gold.'

They went into the study.

'Still, I was a little surprised, I must say,' the dean continued. 'I am naturally a keen student of human nature – all doctors are – and after all I inflicted on him it would have needed the disinterestedness of a well-established saint so generously to save my bacon. And my knighthood.'

'Lionel – ' She bit her lip. 'He did it because of me.'

'He's always been very fond of you, of course.'

'Lionel – there's something I must tell you.' The dean stared at her. 'Do you remember, in the summer of 1953, when I said I couldn't stand the crowds in London for the Coronation? I left the children with you and nanny, to stay in the country with my sister for a fortnight. Well, I didn't stay with her. Not for a fortnight, anyway. For one of the weeks – it was the fourth week in May – I went away with Lancelot. To Le Touquet. I remember it vividly every time I hear that tune "I've Never Been In Love Before", from *Guys and Dolls*.'

'Good God! You mean to say that you – ?'

'I'm afraid so, Lionel.'

'You were…?'

'I'm very much afraid so, Lionel.'

'By *Lancelot*?'

'I'm afraid that I *was*, Lionel.'

The dean shook his head slowly. 'I'd better gum up those pages in the disciplinary committee minute-book again.'

Richard Gordon

Doctor in the House

Richard Gordon's acceptance into St Swithin's medical school came as no surprise to anyone, least of all him – after all, he had been to public school, played first XV rugby, and his father was, let's face it, 'a St Swithin's man'. Surely he was set for life. It was rather a shock then to discover that, once there, he would actually have to work, and quite hard. Fortunately for Richard Gordon, life proved not to be all dissection and textbooks after all… This hilarious hospital comedy is perfect reading for anyone who's ever wondered exactly what medical students get up to in their training. Just don't read it on your way to the doctor's!

'Uproarious, extremely iconoclastic' – *Evening News*
'A delightful book' – *Sunday Times*

Doctor at Sea

Richard Gordon's life was moving rapidly towards middle-aged lethargy – or so he felt. Employed as an assistant in general practice – the medical equivalent of a poor curate – and having been 'persuaded' that marriage is as much an obligation for a young doctor as celibacy for a priest, Richard sees the rest of his life stretching before him. Losing his nerve, and desperately in need of an antidote, he instead signs on with the Fathom Steamboat Company. What follows is a hilarious tale of nautical diseases and assorted misadventures at sea. Yet he also becomes embroiled in a mystery – what is in the Captain's stomach remedy? And more to the point, what on earth happened to the previous doctor?

'Sheer unadulterated fun' – *Star*

RICHARD GORDON

DOCTOR AT LARGE

Dr Richard Gordon's first job after qualifying takes him to St Swithin's where he is enrolled as Junior Casualty House Surgeon. However, some rather unfortunate incidents with Mr Justice Hopwood, as well as one of his patients inexplicably coughing up nuts and bolts, mean that promotion passes him by – and goes instead to Bingham, his odious rival. After a series of disastrous interviews, Gordon cuts his losses and visits a medical employment agency. To his disappointment, all the best jobs have already been snapped up, but he could always turn to general practice…

DOCTOR GORDON'S CASEBOOK

'Well, I see no reason why anyone should expect a doctor to be on call seven days a week, twenty-four hours a day. Considering the sort of risky life your average GP leads, it's not only inhuman but simple-minded to think that a doctor could stay sober that long…'

As Dr Richard Gordon joins the ranks of such world-famous diarists as Samuel Pepys and Fanny Burney, his most intimate thoughts and confessions reveal the life of a GP to be not quite as we might expect… Hilarious, riotous and just a bit too truthful, this is Richard Gordon at his best.

RICHARD GORDON

GREAT MEDICAL DISASTERS

Man's activities have been tainted by disaster ever since the serpent first approached Eve in the garden. And the world of medicine is no exception. In this outrageous and strangely informative book, Richard Gordon explores some of history's more bizarre medical disasters. He creates a catalogue of mishaps including anthrax bombs on Gruinard Island, destroying mosquitoes in Panama, and Mary the cook who, in 1904, inadvertently spread Typhoid across New York State. As the Bible so rightly says, 'He that sinneth before his maker, let him fall into the hands of the physician.'

THE PRIVATE LIFE OF JACK THE RIPPER

In this remarkably shrewd and witty novel, Victorian London is brought to life with a compelling authority. Richard Gordon wonderfully conveys the boisterous, often lusty panorama of life for the very poor – hard, menial work; violence; prostitution; disease. *The Private Life of Jack The Ripper* is a masterly evocation of the practice of medicine in 1888 – the year of Jack the Ripper. It is also a dark and disturbing medical mystery. Why were his victims so silent? And why was there so little blood?

'…horribly entertaining…excitement and suspense buttressed with authentic period atmosphere' – *The Daily Telegraph*

TITLES BY RICHARD GORDON AVAILABLE DIRECT
FROM HOUSE OF STRATUS

Quantity		£	$(US)	$(CAN)	€
	THE CAPTAIN'S TABLE	6.99	11.50	15.99	11.50
	DOCTOR AND SON	6.99	11.50	15.99	11.50
	DOCTOR AT LARGE	6.99	11.50	15.99	11.50
	DOCTOR AT SEA	6.99	11.50	15.99	11.50
	DOCTOR IN CLOVER	6.99	11.50	15.99	11.50
	DOCTOR IN LOVE	6.99	11.50	15.99	11.50
	DOCTOR IN THE HOUSE	6.99	11.50	15.99	11.50
	DOCTOR IN THE NEST	6.99	11.50	15.99	11.50
	DOCTOR IN THE NUDE	6.99	11.50	15.99	11.50
	DOCTOR IN THE SOUP	6.99	11.50	15.99	11.50
	DOCTOR IN THE SWIM	6.99	11.50	15.99	11.50
	DOCTOR ON THE BALL	6.99	11.50	15.99	11.50
	DOCTOR ON THE BRAIN	6.99	11.50	15.99	11.50
	DOCTOR ON THE JOB	6.99	11.50	15.99	11.50
	DOCTOR ON TOAST	6.99	11.50	15.99	11.50
	DOCTOR'S DAUGHTERS	6.99	11.50	15.99	11.50
	DR GORDON'S CASEBOOK	6.99	11.50	15.99	11.50
	THE FACEMAKER	6.99	11.50	15.99	11.50
	GOOD NEIGHBOURS	6.99	11.50	15.99	11.50

ALL HOUSE OF STRATUS BOOKS ARE AVAILABLE FROM GOOD BOOKSHOPS OR
DIRECT FROM THE PUBLISHER:

Internet: www.houseofstratus.com including author interviews, reviews, features.

Email: sales@houseofstratus.com please quote author, title and credit card details.

TITLES BY RICHARD GORDON AVAILABLE DIRECT
FROM HOUSE OF STRATUS

Quantity		£	$(US)	$(CAN)	€
☐	GREAT MEDICAL DISASTERS	6.99	11.50	15.99	11.50
☐	GREAT MEDICAL MYSTERIES	6.99	11.50	15.99	11.50
☐	HAPPY FAMILIES	6.99	11.50	15.99	11.50
☐	INVISIBLE VICTORY	6.99	11.50	15.99	11.50
☐	LOVE AND SIR LANCELOT	6.99	11.50	15.99	11.50
☐	NUTS IN MAY	6.99	11.50	15.99	11.50
☐	THE SUMMER OF SIR LANCELOT	6.99	11.50	15.99	11.50
☐	SURGEON AT ARMS	6.99	11.50	15.99	11.50
☐	THE PRIVATE LIFE OF DR CRIPPEN	6.99	11.50	15.99	11.50
☐	THE PRIVATE LIFE OF FLORENCE NIGHTINGALE	6.99	11.50	15.99	11.50
☐	THE PRIVATE LIFE OF JACK THE RIPPER	6.99	11.50	15.99	11.50

ALL HOUSE OF STRATUS BOOKS ARE AVAILABLE FROM GOOD BOOKSHOPS OR
DIRECT FROM THE PUBLISHER:

Hotline: UK ONLY: 0800 169 1780, please quote author, title and credit card details.
INTERNATIONAL: +44 (0) 20 7494 6400, please quote author, title and
credit card details.

Send to: **House of Stratus Sales Department**
24c Old Burlington Street
London
W1X 1RL
UK

Please allow for postage costs charged per order plus an amount per book as set out in the tables below:

	£(Sterling)	$(US)	$(CAN)	€(Euros)
Cost per order				
UK	2.00	3.00	4.50	3.30
Europe	3.00	4.50	6.75	5.00
North America	3.00	4.50	6.75	5.00
Rest of World	3.00	4.50	6.75	5.00
Additional cost per book				
UK	0.50	0.75	1.15	0.85
Europe	1.00	1.50	2.30	1.70
North America	2.00	3.00	4.60	3.40
Rest of World	2.50	3.75	5.75	4.25

PLEASE SEND CHEQUE, POSTAL ORDER (STERLING ONLY), EUROCHEQUE, OR INTERNATIONAL MONEY ORDER (PLEASE CIRCLE METHOD OF PAYMENT YOU WISH TO USE)
MAKE PAYABLE TO: STRATUS HOLDINGS plc

Cost of book(s): ——————— Example: 3 x books at £6.99 each: £20.97

Cost of order: ——————— Example: £2.00 (Delivery to UK address)

Additional cost per book: ——————— Example: 3 x £0.50: £1.50

Order total including postage: ——————— Example: £24.47

Please tick currency you wish to use and add total amount of order:

☐ £ (Sterling)   ☐ $ (US)   ☐ $ (CAN)   ☐ € (EUROS)

VISA, MASTERCARD, SWITCH, AMEX, SOLO, JCB:

☐ ☐ ☐ ☐ ☐ ☐ ☐ ☐ ☐ ☐ ☐ ☐ ☐ ☐ ☐ ☐ ☐ ☐ ☐ ☐

Issue number (Switch only):

☐ ☐ ☐

Start Date: **Expiry Date:**

☐☐ / ☐☐   ☐☐ / ☐☐

Signature: ————————————

NAME: ——————————————————————

ADDRESS: ——————————————————————

——————————————————————

POSTCODE: ————————

Please allow 28 days for delivery.

Prices subject to change without notice.
Please tick box if you do not wish to receive any additional information. ☐

House of Stratus publishes many other titles in this genre; please check our website (**www.houseofstratus.com**) for more details.